Marketing and promotion will include a national
media campaign, bookseller/librarian outreach,
digital advertising, targeted newsletters,
social posts, and giveaways.

For more information, contact:
Rachel Fershleiser, Associate Publisher,
Executive Director of Marketing
rachel.fershleiser@catapult.co

WOO
WOO

ALSO BY ELLA BAXTER

New Animal

WOO WOO

A NOVEL

ELLA BAXTER

CATAPULT NEW YORK

WOO WOO

Copyright © 2024 by Ella Baxter

First Catapult edition: 2024

ISBN: 978-1-64622-255-1

Library of Congress Control Number: TK

Jacket design by Nicole Caputo
Jacket art © iStock / akinbostanci
Book design by Olenka Burgess

Catapult
New York, NY
books.catapult.co

Printed in the United States of America

1 3 5 7 9 10 8 6 4 2

For Nicky

WOO
WOO

This Is Not a Love Song

—PUBLIC IMAGE LTD, 1983

Sabine had traumatised only a few people in her life and one of them was her husband. She stood in their back garden and waited for Constantine to remove the camera from the tripod. It was Monday night. It was about to storm. The sun had set hours ago, and dinnertime had come and gone without mention.

"A reminder that we're aiming for stark and otherworldly," said Sabine. Despite her tone, she was not too dictatorial.

"The sky is actually purple," said Constantine. He held his hand out, palm up, and looked at the cloud overhead.

Sabine unbuttoned her vinyl coat, smoothed her hair back behind her ears, and crouched at the base of their fruiting lemon tree, ready to be immortalised. These photos would be used to publicise her upcoming solo art exhibition. She loved seeing herself named as the photographer for any promotional material. Differentiating herself, no matter how subtly, from the other artists represented by the Goethe Gallery soothed her to no end.

Sabine had briefed Constantine on the importance of capturing the glossiness of her hair and her lively sanpaku eyes. Two aesthetics she was unwilling to compromise on. She'd demonstrated how she would dip her head at a severe angle so that a distinct white gap showed between her iris and the lower lid of her eye. Their garden needed to look untamed and junglelike in the background. The sky must be a deep navy. No stars! And.

"Get some of the lemons in," said Sabine. It was imperative that the waxy lemons were lurid against all that green.

"*Please*," said Constantine.

"Please," said Sabine.

The foliage above and behind Sabine was lit by an industrial floodlight which sat at Constantine's feet and pointed directly at her head. There was no time to disperse the insects or style the lemons. There was no time at all. Her bushy, bleached eyebrows and tall, plump body were in the process of becoming art.

Sabine shifted through a series of poses, tossing her hair, angling her arms, opening her mouth, and tilting her head back, while Constantine moved around the garden capturing her.

"I'm getting sexual art alien. I'm getting a revolution in a body. I'm getting pure genius," said Constantine.

"What else?" said Sabine.

Constantine was shorter and more nuggety than her, with strong legs like a touring camel. He was quick and elegant, moving seamlessly through various squats and stretches as he photographed her. Sabine loved his salted, wiry hair, his defined cheekbones, and his soft paunch. She found her husband's body irresistibly dense.

"You need to make sure I'm mysterious and powerful and surprised, but the portrait also needs to have the emotional impact of *Rip my heart out You Fucking Cunt* by Tracey Emin."

She motioned for Constantine to stop and went over to him, scrolling through her Instagram feed, angling the phone screen towards him as she rolled through reels of pictures.

"Am I framing it wrong? Should I reattach the camera to the tripod?" Constantine held her four-thousand-dollar camera in three fingers of one hand, the strap twisting in the breeze.

"Pure, uncompromising rigour is needed to make transcendent, supernatural art," said Sabine.

"Hear! Hear!" said Constantine.

She returned to the tree, flapped her coat out behind her, and let the light blanch her white skin to ghost.

Constantine held down the shutter button and let more photos accumulate.

"I am impregnating every image with my unruly, creative juju. Are you getting my full body in?" said Sabine.

"You're stunning," said Constantine. He zoomed in.

"The shoes?" said Sabine.

"Devastating," said Constantine. He pointed the camera at her shoes and took a photograph, just of them.

"The eyes?" said Sabine.

"Perfect, in an unexpected way," said Constantine.

Sabine's upcoming exhibition, titled *Fuck You, Help Me*, in simple terms, was fifteen photographic portraits of her swinging naked from things outside at night and one short film; in more complex terms, it was something about discomfort and vulnerability and archetypes. *Something*, Sabine was sure, *about juxtaposition*. In each photograph she was covered from head to toe in sheer costumes. These wearable puppets, several feet long and made from panels of stretch silk, featured silicone faces that Sabine could position over her own. Think of the collection as: blinding flashes of light across a defiant, nude cis-female body. Think: a backdrop of forbidden, murky urban nightscapes.

"Sabine, you need to breathe," said Constantine.

Their usual ritual on Monday nights was for Sabine to burn two salmon fillets, and for Constantine to insist they were delicious. He would swoop in and happily eat his up, even though the blackened fish tasted truly carcinogenic. The other six nights of the week he worked as a chef at one of the busiest restaurants in the city. He returned home late, filthy and exhausted, and smelling of sautéed chicken hearts and ninety-dollar steak.

Constantine put down the camera and extended his hand, and when she took it, he drew her close. He danced her across the grass and then dipped his glorious, emotional, hardworking wife headfirst towards the worm farm until she was cradled in the crook of his arm. She rested there, silent, seeming to enjoy it. After a moment he eased her back to standing.

Constantine's phone rang from his pocket. He held his hand over it, kissed Sabine briefly on the cheek, then entered the house, speaking softly into the phone receiver.

Inside, he slunk past the window, opened the fridge door, and burrowed through the crisper. He snapped leaves off a head of lettuce then leaned against the counter and crunched through them. He hung up the call, pulled a strip of beef jerky from a pantry jar, and ate it in two bites. Shook out a handful of smoked almonds, and tossed them into his mouth. He kept going, running a tablespoon through a block of unsalted butter and dipping it in the salt dish before putting it into his mouth. He took a sip of whisky from the bottle, and then another.

Sabine knew that none of her demands, from the impractical to the perfectionist, were new to Constantine. The last time he had assisted her was on the seven-minute short film to be featured in her exhibition. *Worship Me* began with her taking off her pants and sitting in a dish of animal blood, and ended with her squat-hopping, bare-arsed, along a line of puckered prosthetic lips made from acrylic resin. Sabine had roped Constantine into sourcing the blood through his restaurant's suppliers. For twelve hours, he'd stored that bin bag of blood in the work fridge, and at the end of his shift he'd carried it home, on the bus. And when Sabine, over the following two weeks, kept unknotting the bag and emptying it slowly to rehearse with, he became so upset due to her defiance of all health and safety regulations that he'd threatened to pour it down the drain himself. *Why not practise with water?* he kept asking. *The chef in me can't stand to see all of this waste!*

The temperature dropped and hail began to fall in streamers of white. The balls of ice scattered across the garden and bounced off the metal drains like coins. Sabine gathered the equipment under one arm and hurried inside.

She skirted the end of the leather sofa in their open-plan living room and walked up the hallway, past three double windows, to her studio. Their freestanding worker's cottage was set back in a sulk from the main road. A deep foundational crack had recently formed in one wall, and Sabine traced it with a finger as she walked. Often at this time of night she was distracted from her work by the family of heavyset possums

thumping across the roof, or the pneumatic *tsss* of buses brak-
ing as they pulled into the stop by the front gate. But for now,
only occasional thunderclaps interrupted the torrential hail.

Sabine placed her gear next to a pile of prosthetic noses
and ears that looked like a cubist Greek chorus emerging from
the wood of her desk. Behind her hung the gothic skins, each
of them made to look like alternate versions of herself. Sabine
kept all eighty of them clipped to hooks by the back of their
necks, their heavy prosthetic-laden faces tipped away from
the walls like pissed bel canto singers. Her own valley of the
uncanny. Sabine would have preferred to drape her art around
the house, but the puppets unnerved Constantine. The flutter-
ing eyes and retractable tongues, and the amount of long hair
that she hand-stitched onto their soft, loose heads, were too
much for him. Once, during an argument, he had referred to
them as *snakes in wigs*. Sabine had tried to explain to Constantine that the skins weren't her but they were also *very much*
her. She liked to bring them out for photo shoots then leave
them for a while, either stuffed with pillows and propped up
at the dining table or lying on the bed, but Constantine would
gather them up and drag them back to her studio. It took every ounce of self-control for Sabine not to follow him in her
overalls and bra, fighting him like a dog. She would never disrespect his knives like that.

Sabine uploaded the memory card from her camera to her
laptop, then double-clicked on the folder and leaned forward.
Her breathing slowed. She looked at each portrait with the in-
tensity of a new mother. The floodlight had worked. Her face
looked eerie and possessed. She relaxed. They were good.

She squinted. *Were they good?*

Sabine scrolled to the beginning to look through them

again. The photos were excellent. Her promotional photos would be somewhere among them. She relaxed her shoulders. Bones somewhere in her upper skeleton clicked.

Art, Sabine tweeted, *is my life*. There was so much more to say but that would do for now.

As the hail momentarily eased, Sabine closed down her computer and joined Constantine in the kitchen. She took a large sip of his whisky then raised the bottle towards him.

"To art," said Sabine.

"To both our careers," said Constantine.

"And to us," Sabine added. She took another drink then stoppered the bottle.

With a mouth full of the smoky brine, Sabine approached her husband, cupped his face with her hands, and brought his mouth to hers. She kissed him. A dank and grateful peat-bog single-cask kiss that she hoped would act like a drawstring, cinching them together. She wanted to be encased by his thick arms. She wanted nothing more than for Constantine to meet her with his own open-lotus heart. She lingered near him. Constantine stepped back. Again, his phone rang and he left the kitchen to take another call from the restaurant.

Sabine wasn't hungry. She stacked the cups and plates in the dishwasher, grounding herself in a mundane task. Being domestic was necessary to fuel creativity, as was being strategic, but no one ever wanted to speak to a female artist about these things. Sabine wiped down the kitchen counter in big wet arcs, then squeezed out the sponge until her fist shook and mottled.

In bed, Sabine traced a line down Constantine's spine, from the base of his neck to the top of his tailbone. She mapped each rib that connected to his back and stretched over his side. She missed him. Recently they had both been on a roll of late nights and early mornings. Sabine would not have been surprised if a psychic had told her that the elusive golden goose of success had gobbled them both down, and now she and Constantine were being pushed out, two shiny eggs of capitalist glory. The consequences of his recent promotion to head chef confused Sabine. It was as if his stress had tripled in size. Instead of being gone the usual fifty to sixty hours a week, he was away much longer. Eighty hours a week? One hundred?

Like a mountain climber approaching the summit, she needed three points of contact with her husband at all times. She needed hours of open-ended discussions about intimacy. Let him name in perfect detail all the ways they could twist together. Lambrusco evenings. Genital gazing.

Constantine twitched away from her finger and Sabine folded her hand back and tucked it under her pillow. It would also not surprise her if a psychic told her that she had known her husband in a past life in which they had been feuding lords. There was a sense of ancient tension and mistrust between them. Sabine rested her forehead on her husband's back.

"Your emotional support is my lifeline during the lead-up to my exhibitions. But our closeness fluctuates, do you agree?" said Sabine. "Do you feel it come and go?"

Constantine nodded. "I feel it."

Sabine narrowed her eyes. "But what do you feel?"

"Mainly, I just feel that I love you," said Constantine.

"Yes, me too," she said. "But soulmate connection, mutual awareness, hourly commitments to synchronicity..."

Constantine rolled onto his back and looked at the ceiling.

"Where do you physically feel my love the most? Where is it located in your body?" said Sabine.

WOO WOO   9

"Probably my chest?" said Constantine.

As Sabine repositioned so that her head rested on his chest, she acknowledged silently to herself, and then aloud, that the audience might hate her exhibition. She envisioned being dropped by the Goethe and Constantine having to financially support her. She would have to spend the next season of her life finding some new profession. Sabine had looked up how long it would take to become an archaeologist, or a lecturer, or an electrician. Six years in most cases. She would be forty-four.

Sabine forced herself to visualise an applauding audience. She mentally turned up the volume of the crowd until she was being aggressively cheered. Her exhibition would sell out within half an hour of opening. Maybe even less. She imagined placing each cadmium-red sold sticker onto the wall beside her artwork. She imagined people grabbing her by the shoulders and shaking her, and calling her work wildly engaging. She rolled onto her stomach and flattened her palms against the mattress, but the tug of gravity sickened her. She flipped over and coughed.

"Sabine," said Constantine, in a tone that told her to stop the nocturnal Cossack dance. He rolled around to face her, put a hand on her shoulder, and held her still.

"Talk to me," he said.

"I father the work and then the public mothers it. Do I want them to be kind and understanding mothers? Sure, a little. Do I want to immediately fill the space I now have spare in my life with fathering more work to maintain career momentum? Not really, but thinking like this is—oh my fucking god." Sabine covered her face with her hands.

"Every person who sees my exhibition is going to have an opinion about it," she moaned. He underestimated how tender she became. Like a piece of sous vide meat, she was extremely softened by the process. The closer the time came for her work to be in the world, the more life force drained out of her in anticipation.

To encourage her to breathe, Constantine asked her to sing to him, but she wanted to know if he thought the puppet skins were interesting and complex, even though she had been making them for the last ten years. Were they still freakishly alluring and current? And, aside from his issue with the procurement of blood, what did he think of the film concept? The film title? Should she pivot entirely to making films? Her whole being registered the devastating anxiety of potential rejection. Raw. Embryonic. Vulnerable. The agony, the pure—

"Sing to me," he said. Sabine dutifully sang the first few lines of "Auld Lang Syne," and when she got to the end of the parts she remembered, Constantine asked her to start again, and she did.

A Fierce and Violent Opening

—DOROTHEA LASKY, 2018

On Tuesday morning, thunder rolled and thudded in the distance but the rain stopped briefly enough for Constantine to dash to work, and for Sabine to walk to the local grocer and back. She took the laneways home, lugging kefir, limes, and a bag of discounted pomegranates so ripe they had split, exposing their glittering seeds.

As Sabine passed the hot chicken shop, she remembered Cecily's request that she use social media heavily during the lead-up to her exhibition. Recording anything with a camera made it into art. She could sit in front of a camera and do nothing and, somehow, through the action of recording, it became a performance. The immediacy of a constant audience was a curse and a gift. She paused in front of the car wash and live streamed herself on TikTok.

"Just jumping on here to talk about the artist's role in reinterpreting the world."

Sabine passed a huge electric sign advertising car wax, which shimmered on top of a peeling building, the massive pixels distorted against the muted sky. There was a skeleton of beauty in her environment, she just had to dig deep enough to see it.

Twelve people joined her live stream.

"My gallerist at the Goethe, Cecily, believes that good art is essentially a critical rewrite of the artist's experience," said Sabine.

She noticed the puffy, pollen-covered legs of bees rump-deep in the flowering vine that grew along the metal fence of the recycling centre. Sabine held her phone close to the bees, showing her followers.

"Also, there's street parking at the gallery if anyone is driving to my exhibition next week," said Sabine.

Behind the fence, abandoned, empty aqua-coloured pools stood upright on their sides. There was an irregular clanging sound from the foundry.

She continued walking beneath transmission lines that ran like staples between the car-wrecking yards, wig wholesalers, and custom-made bathroom factories. They lived in the outer north of Melbourne. Constantine loved the area. His mother lived there. His nonna too. He bought wine grapes to make Dolcetto, and barrels of olives, from an Italian man, five doors down. Sabine tolerated the suburban-dry-grass quiet. Sometimes, she even let herself believe that it made her ideas louder.

"Anyway, let me reinterpret and rewrite my environment to you. I smell cement dust and burnt rubber, freshly laid bitumen and diesel fumes from the nearby earthworks. I am surrounded by a cacophony of small gods, each of them worthy of attention, but none of them particularly holy," said Sabine.

She trailed one hand across a cyclone fence, keeping the phone close to capture the sound.

Bubble_Thumper commented: *Yes girl give us nothing*

Dexie_Chicks commented: *Bébé how will you spend the portrait prize money?*

UdonPoodle commented: *Go back to the bee again. Into it*

"Should I do a Q and A live? Leave your questions in the comments," said Sabine.

Candle_in_the_bin commented: *Do you have any suggestions for how to get gallery representation?*

MetalLord commented: *Why are you still using silicone when we are in an environmental crisis? You could make your creatures in biodegradable materials*

Dexie_Chicks commented: *They're not creatures!? They are sculptures of disfigured women. No disrespect*

Bubble_Thumper commented: *No they're self-portraits and she's been making them for years*

MetalLord commented: *The puppet of Baba Yaga with legs of horse bones is a self-portrait???*

UdonPoodle commented: *Yes*

Dexie_Chicks commented: *Yes*

VeneratedSuperSaint commented: *Go home*

Double_XL_FeverBitch commented: *Her grandmother on her dad's side is Slavic so it's ok*

UdonPoodle commented: *She's already said she will try and address the bioethics at some point*

Sabine frowned at her screen.

"Okay, well, my loves, I must get back to reinterpreting my world. I appreciate you!" She turned the camera around to face her, held it to her mouth, and kissed them goodbye.

At home, Sabine spent a serious amount of the afternoon

arranging the pomegranates along the dining table, resting
on their stalks. She had until around midnight to work on the
logistics of her exhibition. Then Constantine would return
home, his beard dotted with beads of rendered fat, his feet
aching from hours in rubber clogs. He harboured a constant
fear of falling over in the kitchen.

She photographed the pomegranates, rearranged them,
and took more photographs. She then took a break, sitting
on a rusted chair at the back of the garden where creeping
vines as thick as brambles fell over the fence into the rear
lane in loose piles. Smoking from her emergency packet of
cigarettes, she nestled herself between taro, chocolate mint,
yuccas, deadheading the plants closest to her.

The neighbours' gardens were neat and planned. Trimmed
and wood-chipped. How great. Five stars. In her garden, she
let the plants grow how the plants wanted to grow, and they
loved her for it. Packets of seeds that Sabine had shaken hap-
hazardly over the ground now bloomed around her in shocking colours.

Part of Sabine's artistic process was letting the process
unfold however it liked. Part of her process was simply being
aware that a process was taking place. Back inside the house,
Sabine opened her computer with every intention of at least
beginning her artist statement for the exhibition, but an hour
later she was deep into photo albums of old holidays. She remembered doing nothing then too.

Once the sun had set, she opened a bottle of plum wine and
ate the plums, read a poetry book, and crunched through one-
third of a jar of walnuts. She napped. Bathed. Played a maria-
chi record. Ate half a salty supermarket quiche.

Ruth rang. "Tell me you're coming to Lou's dinner party."

Ruth was Sabine's best friend from art school. She was also an artist with the Goethe Gallery. Ruth, who had platinum-blond hair and muscular arms, was in love with Lou, who was an integral part of the Melbourne art scene. He and his friends attended all the important openings at the Goethe. Most of his group were up-and-coming artists, pouring into the art scene from postgraduate degrees. They wore clothes from the mid-nineties—big pants and small tops—and had home tattoos. Lou exclusively wore clothing made from ripstop fabrics; that, and his German heritage, made him look rock climber adjacent. Perpetually midway through his PhD on the artifice of something in a particular time period, Lou had once told Sabine that her art was *chronically and unselfconsciously online*, a comment that was impossible for her to decipher.

"I feel dated next to them. They are fearless; all the leaking glow sticks and anti-art. Remember the group exhibition, *Low-Fat Violet*, the one where Nafeesa created a bed from empty packets of temazepam?" said Sabine.

"*Low-Fat Violet* changed my life," said Ruth.

"It was too good," said Sabine.

Sabine walked to the bedroom and upended two baskets of clothes. On the bed, she laid out a tube top and high-waisted pants, but she couldn't accept the pinkness of the top. It was a Palm Beach pink. Millennial pink. Burgundy was what she needed to wear right now. Mulled wine. Autumnal leaves. The fuzzy edge of a Rothko. Beef. Bruises. Rhubarb. Roses. Blood clots. Serious, authoritative burgundy.

"I have nothing to wear," said Sabine.

"Wear the jumpsuit with the pockets," said Ruth.

Sabine burrowed through her drawers. She tossed a scarf

over her shoulder, followed by a hat. She hauled out a series
of single leather gloves, and then slapped each of them onto
the floor. She needed so much (wine, encouragement, reas-
surance) but she was unable to voice her needs because she
couldn't focus on anything beyond the maddening pink and
the unbearable weight that she would endure as a successful
artist in a room full of more interesting graduates.

Her needs went unmet. She gave up on finding the jumpsuit and snapped on the top and pants instead, then stood
back from the mirror, her head to one side. Rolling the dice,
Sabine changed into a slip and cowboy boots.

"I'm dressed, I'm coming. But I'll leave early if everyone is
wearing tabis and doing nangs," said Sabine.

"Me too," said Ruth.

Mutiny by Maison Margiela

—NADIA LEE COHEN, 2019

It was Ruth who opened the door, wearing tabis.

"You're finally here," Ruth gushed. "Come in. Get warm. Don't tell him I love him and don't ask about his PhD."

Sabine surveyed that evening's dinner-party tundra. Lou lived in a large Victorian terrace near Gertrude Street. Their share house furniture was sparse. Rush-seated chairs. Fairy lights. An unbelievable number of indoor plants.

The guests milled around the long dining table. In the centre, fruit-shaped candles rested on glass saucers. Melting pineapples. Bananas on fire. Surrounding the candles were several bottles of wine, which were opened in a cannon by another woman with bleached eyebrows.

These dinner parties made Sabine think of Félix González-Torres's famous artwork *"Untitled" (Portrait of Ross in L.A.)*, which was essentially seventy-nine kilos of lollies dropped in

the corner of an art gallery. The mound of sugar represented
the weight of the artist's dead lover, and as people passed
by they would take a piece and eat it, slowly and obliviously
consuming Ross's body. For Sabine, hours of communal eating and being talked at about art was the equivalent of being
slowly eroded. She was always braced for Lou's friends, the
kids, to ask her questions. She felt that, as an established artist
who had won grants and exhibited internationally, it would be
only natural for them to seek her opinions on their portfolios
or exhibitions. Sabine had been preparing to give advice for
years, but the entreaties never came.

Ruth, seemingly impervious to the stress of being surrounded by emerging artists, helped herself to a wedge of ooz-
ing brie, withered muscatel grapes and burnt-orange quince
paste. She poured Sabine a wine and then handed her the
wineglass. Sabine gripped the stem, barely able to hear whatever Ruth was saying, let alone her own thoughts. She was too
fixated on everyone's exquisite mullets.

Lou and his flatmates took turns hosting these dinner parties. Sabine regularly liked the pictures they posted on Instagram of jammy Chantilly cakes and layered jellies. They were
named Kiki, Gregor, Octavia or Martin. The Rumis and the
Clovers and the Kits all synchronising the exhales of their fat
plumes of vape, filling the room with grey clouds of chilli-lime
mango, wafts of gummy bear and Caramilk e-juice.

Without even turning her head she could see no fewer
than three navel piercings. Her mother's voice in her head:
Where did they find these clothes? Von Dutch. Juicy Couture.
The North Face. Their androgyny and their playfulness. Hairy
armpits and thin eyebrows. There was a loose thread trailing

from the hem of Sabine's dress. She tore it off. And it was clear
that *everyone* had brought wine.

"Was I supposed to bring wine? You said not to bring anything," said Sabine.

The bottles displayed alluring, detailed labels. Dark wine
with corks. Sabine sipped. It was good wine. How did the children afford this wine?

"Don't worry, there's plenty," said Ruth.

"Is anyone here getting signed to the Goethe?" said Sabine.

"Probably half of them," said Ruth.

"Who?" said Sabine.

Ruth pointed out five people.

Sabine took a moment to stare at each of the kids who were
chomping at her heels. She recognised a twenty-five-year-old
oil painter who used baroque techniques and who also internationally exhibited. As Sabine looked on, the girl bent over,
revealing a Rugrats tattoo on her lower back.

"Oh, it can't be," said Sabine.

"No one here makes edible sculptures," said Ruth, "so I'm
pretty safe."

Ruth was famous—in Melbourne at least—for her work,
which occupied the intersection between baking and marine
life. She made cakes that looked like whales, which she then
threw at gallery walls. When Ruth picked up her cake whales
and chucked them, it was as if she were splitting the atom.
There was machismo and meaning to her art. She partnered
with Greenpeace and some other NGO, so all her shows got
write-ups. She had the enviable accessory of a cause. Her artist statements wrote themselves: Helping whales. Visibility.
Endangerment. Global warming. The horror of human force.

The cakes were vegan. They were ethical cakes.

"Who explores film? Portraits? Anything nude?" said Sabine. "Or puppets?" she added.

Ruth pointed to a woman wearing a white tennis skirt and a jumper with the words *Modern Fart* embroidered on it. "She made the film *Would You Ever Get Punched in the Sternum for Free?* That was pretty close to you."

My art? Sabine gulped her wine. *Look at her, she hates art!*

A day earlier, Sabine had sent Ruth digital files of the exhibition, which Ruth had responded to with a series of emojis. Skulls and leaves, stars and thick red exclamation points. Hieroglyphs that Sabine hadn't been able to decipher.

"What did you think of my exhibition photos?" said Sabine. She stared at Ruth's inscrutable face. Ruth parted her lips as if she were about to say something, then closed them and cleared her throat.

"What is it?" she said. "Be as honest as you can."

Ruth inhaled. "I think it's some of your best work."

"Some of?" said Sabine.

"They are very effective portraits and I love the faces," said Ruth, finally.

Sabine pushed her index fingers into each tear duct. "Do you mean you think their faces are intriguing or disturbing?" She added, "I'm finding it hard to unpack your use of *effective*, if I'm honest." She placed a hand over her mouth to stop any more words from coming out. The acidity of disappointment ran through her. The heaviness of shame pulled her flat.

"I said I love them," said Ruth, looking stressed.

"Is it that you think I'm challenging the viewer too much? Am I asking too much of my audience?"

"You're not listening to me," said Ruth. "They are instantly appealing."

She suffered while Ruth murdered her with brutal, unchecked honesty. Death by a thousand cuts. Sabine sank deep down, lead boots to the bottom of the Atlantic.

"They're really good," said Ruth, nodding her head for emphasis.

Sabine mentally calculated what the exhibition had cost her so far. There would be time to fix it. The paper was recyclable.

"You always worry at this stage in the process," said Ruth. "You work and work and then you step back and think, *I'm a failure. I should die.* Art is abusive."

"No one will care about me hanging off things and ass-printing blood. It's boring," said Sabine. This was not New York. She was not Jeff Koons.

"No one cares until they care," said Ruth.

Lou presented them with a silver tray of Pringles fanned around a ramekin of taramosalata. Sabine took four, pre-dipping and stacking each chip on her open palm. She chewed on them like a rat.

"Was I supposed to bring wine?" said Sabine.

"It's totally fine," said Lou.

"Did Ruth show you the exhibition files?" said Sabine.

"Interesting use of flash," said Lou.

"Ten thousand lumens," said Sabine.

"You're lucky you get away with so much. I would be crucified by Cecily if I started making nude art with profanities in the title," said Ruth.

"Luck is mostly privilege," said Lou.

"Luck is real," said Sabine.

"You're both white," said Lou.

"Well, then you're more privileged than us, being a white man," said Ruth.

"I'm trans. You need to read a book," said Lou.

"You're absolutely right," said Sabine, immediately ready to prove herself a greater ally than Ruth.

"It may be an age thing, but compared to most people here, I have a really clear understanding of my own art in relation to all the artists who have come before me," said Sabine. "Would you say that anyone here knows which artist attempted to breathe water, or locked themselves in a room with a wild dog, or let the audience assault her and spiritually demean her?"

"I'm curious as to why this matters to you," said Lou.

"I need to rejuvenate. I need to take risks," said Sabine.

"What about including more layers in your work? I could see you taking your alter egos in a dreamier direction. The puppets have the potential to be more enchanting. Look at the work of Min Jia or Mimosa Echard. Is the feminism that underpins your art intersectional? Are you observing other artists? Are you going to shows?" said Lou.

"You can't get more dreamy than naked self-portraits," said Sabine.

"Do you know of Puppies Puppies?" said Lou.

"Rings a bell," said Sabine.

"Chidinma Nnoli?" said Lou.

"Probably," said Sabine.

"Their work is fresh," said Lou.

Sabine took a long sip. She would die to be fresh.

"Double down on being online. Look at the formula of

memes and vines, really lean into deep viral internet culture," said Lou.

He showed Sabine a picture of a border collie whose head had been photoshopped into a stalk of broccoli; beneath the picture was the word *Brocollie*. One by one the other guests came over and wheezed with laughter.

Lou excused himself to return to the kitchen, and Sabine tried to think about the critical discourse around vulnerability in art, but her thoughts were too slippery to hold. A petite woman with hard nipples bumped into Sabine. They turned to apologise to each other.

"The vibes are immaculate," the petite woman said. She circled her finger, gesturing to the music. "Smooth Operator" by Sade played. Sabine told the petite woman that Sade was a style icon. Sabine explained that throughout her life she'd tried to copy Sade's exact fashion aesthetic. The petite woman told Sabine it was such a shame that Sade had died. Sabine informed her that Sade absolutely wasn't dead.

"I'm in a group show, you should come by. It's basically everyone who graduated last year from the imagination workshops," said the petite woman.

Let it not be called Metamorphosis, thought Sabine.

"The show is called *Metamorphosis*," said the petite woman.

"Ruth!" said Sabine. She craned her neck looking for her friend.

Sabine found Ruth at the doorway to the kitchen, openly admiring Lou as he grated green papaya into a mixing bowl and tossed it with his hands.

"Are they laughing at us?" Sabine asked Ruth.

"It's just how they talk," said Ruth.

The wine and candles were cleared away and replaced with a steel pot of massaman curry. Piles of noodles garnished with fresh basil, chopped green chilli, and crunchy, slightly burned, bitter peanuts. A steaming oblong plate of sticky coconut rice covered in torn lime leaves and with a silver spoon driven into the heart of the mound. Hunks of sweet potato rested against soft lamb in a sauce so sweet it could have been a dessert. Sabine added to her plate fried chive cake and green papaya salad with red chilli and halved cherry tomatoes. She tonged rice noodles coated in chilli jam, which she forked into her mouth quicker than an inhale. She ate and ate, lowering her face to her fork, enjoying the way the tamarind created a sour fur across her tongue. On her sixth glass of wine, and after revisiting the Brocollie meme, no more enlightened than the first time she saw it, Sabine ignored the natural direction of the conversation and instead stepped boldly into her own performance of being at a dinner party.

"These forks are so medieval. Lou, you've gone to a huge amount of effort. Where did you learn to cook like this? Sorry, I have to interrupt because, actually. Oh, you're going to review my exhibition? You don't have to. I think there's already enough people who are going to do that. But if you do, and you have questions about my intent, just ask! Don't assume! It's like, my puppets are layered, because I am inside them. Egg and nucleus. You'll find my current exhibition is a typhoon of intersectionality. Yes, I definitely think that. Hey, you know, sorry to interrupt but I'm actually more interested in hearing about your art. Can you repeat that? I swear I was just talking to someone else who was also going to Berlin. Can we get a show of hands of who has recently been? Wunderbar! And did you say galleries are dead? What else is dead? Do you read *Art + Fashion*? Do you have a favourite meme?"

Sabine paused briefly to consider whether her ex-boy-friend, who had once called her a silly little lying bitch, was perhaps right.

Meat Joy

—CAROLEE SCHNEEMANN, 1964

The Uber dropped Sabine home in the rain. The gutters along the street had flooded and so she was forced to leap from the back of the car to the median strip. She squelched over the wet grass towards her house. At the front gate, she stopped briefly. The whole house was lit up, Christmassy bright. The curtains had been pulled open in each room and all the lights were switched on. Sabine checked the time. It was only ten thirty. Constantine wasn't usually home for another hour or so. She unlocked the front door.

"Constantine?" said Sabine. She stepped into the entrance hall. The door slammed shut behind her.

She made her way through the house, turning off each light as she went. In her studio, both the overhead light and lamp were on. She switched them off, then pulled the curtains shut.

"Hello?" said Sabine, walking towards the living room.

No response.

Sabine stopped abruptly at the end of the hallway. From where she stood, she could see through to the belly of the house, the living area. Sabine flinched. In the centre of the kitchen stood a short woman, staring at her. The woman had shoulder-length curly grey hair and oversized owl eyeglasses and wore a loose floral shirt with velvet buttons. On her feet were pristine Asics runners. Sabine took a step backwards.

"Everything is alive and everything has a soul. From a dead pigeon to this awful house," said the woman. She gestured to the room. "Can I ask, do either of you ever clean?"

"You look exactly like Carolee Schneemann," said Sabine.

"I am her," said the woman.

"She's dead," said Sabine.

"I am aware," said the ghost of Carolee Schneemann.

"What's your face doing?" said Sabine, walking towards the ghost until they both stood under the paper lantern light in the kitchen. Carolee's chin multiplied across her face rapidly, with the faintest pinging sound like a slot machine, then disappeared altogether. Sabine tracked the chin, as it slowly reappeared from the bottom of Carolee's face, lengthening and shortening until it found its way back to normal.

"Would it help if I held on to your chin?" said Sabine.

"No. Don't touch me. You've caught me in the process of re-calibration," said Carolee.

"Is this a haunting?" said Sabine.

Carolee pulled out a dining chair, and then sat at the table, both hands resting in her lap.

"Cézanne would love this house," said Carolee. Her eyebrows remained raised. She gripped the edge of the table and crossed her legs.

Sabine slid into the seat opposite. The chin had settled. The face looked right.

"It's all so painterly. The vase of hydrangeas, the linen curtains, the over-stacked fruit bowl," said Carolee. She smiled.

"This is unreal," said Sabine.

"I have to show you something, but before I do that you need to formally ask for my help," said Carolee.

"I mean, you've made some of the most brilliant art," said Sabine.

"You're not wrong," said Carolee.

"The erotic relationship with your cat... the... the images of you—portraits? Where you are wearing just a snake, or shards of glass, or the one where you are biting bones—I've always wondered if they were goat bones? And then the one where you were naked and sliding around with uncooked chicken bodies and..."

"*Meat Joy*," said Carolee.

"Can't have been easy," said Sabine.

Carolee drummed her fingers on the table.

"So this is a mentorship?" said Sabine.

"We can call it that," said Carolee.

"Carolee Schneemann, painter, revolutionary, early pioneer of installation, body politics, and feminist art, and fearless interrogator of performance as body and body as performance, please, can you mentor me?" said Sabine.

"Marvellous," said Carolee. Her neck seemed to bulge and then settle as if she had swallowed something large.

"Everything okay?" said Sabine.

Carolee pointed to the moon. "I'm going to pull your attention here for a moment. Have you noticed how incredibly full it is?"

"I did notice, yes," said Sabine.

"Luminous, would you agree?" said Carolee.

"All right," said Sabine.

"And everything is dandy with me here in this body, right? I look exactly like myself?" Carolee reached up and patted her fingertips over her scalp.

"What's the afterlife like?" said Sabine.

"The sameness of it all hits you like a brick to the head," said Carolee.

"Do you live in a house and make food and see friends?" said Sabine. "What about telekinesis?"

"You are forced to merge into the pool of collected energies. It is like being in the centre of a crowd on a hot day," said Carolee.

"How will the mentorship begin? Should we start by talking about the direction I see my art taking?" said Sabine.

"We are going to look at creating false mayhem—that's true art—but first we must identify the problem," said Carolee. "Come with me."

They stood side by side and stared through the window into the moving garden. Every plant, a conduit for the wind.

"What do you see?" said Carolee.

"I see my beautiful garden," said Sabine.

"Hmm," said Carolee.

Outside, something large sprinted across the yard. Sabine's head snapped up.

Beyond the bushes, a tall shadow darted from one side of the lawn to the other. The shadow swung from a branch of the lemon tree, dropped to the ground, and faced them.

A man.

A Rembrandt portrait with white skin, wide-set brown eyes, and short fluffy hair, his body swathed in black things. Black pants and gloves. *Gloves?* He looked down at his boots, then up to her. He put his hands in his pockets and took a step towards her, and then another.

Sabine recoiled as if bitten, her brain bending in alarm. Her ears roared with blood. Her body was deafening but she returned his gaze, not daring to break eye contact. She burned. Hot ash and pieces of molten metal fell from her. She didn't blink.

The strange man took one hand out of his pocket and pointed at her, then pulled the point into a wave. He smiled. He began to mouth a word—maybe *hello*—but Sabine had already started to move. She pinballed out of the kitchen, through the living room, and down the hallway, shrieking, her feet skidding along the floorboards as she ran, Carolee racing along beside her.

They fell over each other's feet, the hallway not wide enough for both of their strong, impatient bodies. Sabine swore and slowed almost to a stop to let Carolee pass, but Carolee rushed her on.

"Quickly," said Carolee.

"Who was that?" said Sabine.

In the bedroom they faced each other, panting.

"Who is he?" said Sabine.

"Did you know Genghis Khan ordered his soldiers to light three torches each, so his army looked three times the size at night?" said Carolee.

"I need water. I am finding it hard to breathe," said Sabine.

"And now I'm thinking about the bees. You know, if a hive

receives an intruder, the bees gather around that intruder bee and vibrate to generate heat until it dies—it's called 'heat balling,'" said Carolee.

"Did the man look dirty to you? It looked as though he was covered in soil," said Sabine.

"I'm talking to you about subterfuge, about trickery and smoke and mirrors, false mayhem," said Carolee.

"And did you see he was wearing gloves?" said Sabine.

"Did I see? I was staring at his hands thinking the phalanges are the most violent of all our extremities," said Carolee. Her chin sagged, momentarily dragging the rest of her face downwards.

"Would you like a wet cloth for your face?" said Sabine.

"Why? What's it doing now?" said Carolee. Her face snapped back into place.

"No, my mistake. You're all good," said Sabine. The sound of a key turning in a lock startled them.

Carolee tilted her head to listen. "It's your husband."

"Constantine!" said Sabine. She raced past Carolee and flung open the bedroom door.

"There was a man in the back garden and—" she began but he was already dropping his backpack.

"What?" said Constantine.

"And I met—"

Sabine turned around to see if Carolee was behind her, but the bedroom was empty.

"A man? What man? Do we know him?" said Constantine.

"A stranger," said Sabine. She followed Constantine who was already running down the hall.

Sabine stood behind him as he looked through the kitchen window into the moving garden.

"I can't see anyone," said Constantine. "Are you absolutely sure?"

She told him the man had swung from a branch. She pointed her finger to the glass.

"Right there," she said. "He waved to me."

"And you're sure it wasn't a shadow? Or a bat?" It was necessary for him to provide some yang to her constant, thrumming yin. Ideas or worries that she conjured—often in the night—needed to be stemmed. If he allowed himself to be carried along by the current of her river, they would both go headfirst over the edge of her continuous waterfall. Instead he moulded himself into a bridge for her, and then invited her to cross it.

"You know bats love this garden," he said.

Sabine was looking around for weapons. The marble chopping board, secateurs, and the block of knives were all within reach. A grunt escaped from her; there were things to use if needed.

"Go out and check," she said.

"Well," said Constantine. He leaned over the sink and wound open the window. He stuck his hand through the gap. "It's still raining," he said.

The man had waved at her as if he knew her, as if he had been invited over for coffee. He might still be outside watching them deliberate. A fizz of adrenaline rose in Sabine. She pushed in front of her husband, wound the window closed, and locked it.

"Go," she said again, ushering him towards the back door.

Constantine pulled his gardening boots on. He held his hand to his mouth as he yawned.

"Gosh," he said, rubbing his eyes.

Before he left, he took a few sips of water from a small cup. Sabine shrank away to the other side of the room as he lumbered over to the door, opened it wide, and then took three steps into the yard. He returned, shivering as he closed the door.

"Nothing," he said. "Empty."

Satisfied, Constantine headed back to the bedroom, but Sabine remained in the kitchen, her legs planted in front of the sink. She filled the kettle, selected the thickest, longest rolling pin, and took a stalk of lemongrass from the fridge. Holding the rolling pin in both hands, she banged the stalk flat, and kept going as the husk juiced and frayed, turned to mush. The kettle boiled and she put the lemongrass into a teapot and poured in water, filling it to the brim. As she drank the tea she kept watch over the rolling bushes and creaking trees outside.

Eventually a freezing draught filtered like floodwater through the gaps in the floorboards and moved her on. In her studio, she sharpened her pencil to a needle, then opened her journal to a new page and drew the man's body as if made from vines, his fingers as leaves, and his head as a dandelion puffball. She immortalised him on the page, sealing him in graphite.

Sabine looked up the Rembrandt painting titled *Self-Portrait with Dishevelled Hair*. In the painting, Rembrandt had placed muddy apricot and inky green shadows over his face until only the edges of his hair, neck, and ear were visible. The Rembrandt Man in the garden, just as shadowy, had emerged as suddenly as the snowbell flowers, which formed overnight like pearls in a gluggy oyster; but unlike them, he was not welcome. With a green ballpoint pen she drew tendrils of plants crawling out of his ears and nostrils and the corners of his eyeballs. She added thorns and bees, and a wasp nest. She dated the picture, tore it out of her journal, and pinned it to the board above her desk. Next to it were receipts for materials that she had saved for her taxes and a photograph of Ruth faceplanting into her cake on her thirty-seventh birthday, the layers of sponge cracking like wood. Sabine sat back in her chair and listened to the steady wash of rain hitting the roof.

She turned to the next page in her journal and drew the layout of her exhibition in the Goethe Gallery. She made a list of things she still needed to organise. An artist statement. One of the images Constantine had taken of her, uploaded to her website. A lymphatic drainage massage.

Something crunched across the gravel side path outside her studio window. Sabine laid her pencil across her journal and listened. With orb eyes and sodden armpits, she strained to hear. The rain turned to hail again, drowning out any other noise.

Sabine turned off each light on her way to the bedroom, purposely sinking the house into the rest of the night. Every few steps she stopped, craned her head, and listened closely.

The light of the internet modem in the hallway shone into the bedroom. Sabine stood at the foot of the bed, lit in the blue glow, and watched Constantine's hairy stomach rise and fall. One loud cough was enough to wake him. He rolled over with a huff.

"Did you hear anything?" said Sabine.

"Only an anxious woman coughing," said Constantine.

"What if he comes back?" Sabine said.

"I'll tell him to go away," said Constantine. He opened his arms wide. "Come here. Lie on me if you want."

Sabine climbed into bed and curled into his warm butter-body. She matched her breathing to his slow inhale and exhale until she was receiving the equivalent amount of oxygen, both of them opening and closing like two ends of an accordion. She lay there but could not sustain the stillness. She got up once to check the bedroom window was locked, and again to step into the hall, only to look both directions before retreating to bed.

A headache pulsed at her right temple. She needed a glass of water. She got up and tiptoed to the kitchen. She drank the water over the sink, washed her glass, and stacked it away. For a moment she stood in the dark and watched as the greenery of the garden bounced hypnotically. It beckoned her.

Outside, dressed in her robe and cowboy boots, Sabine stood under the lemon tree and let the white noise of the night butt against her. Her thoughts grew from a cavalry to a stampede.

She unwound the garden hose, pointed the nozzle at the branch of the tree the man had touched, and shot water along the smooth bark. She turned off the hose, dumped it nose-first into a bush, and then pulled her phone out of the waistband of her robe. She leaned the phone against the kitchen window, pressed record, and stood in front of it.

Sabine assumed the watchful expression of the man. She lifted her hand to point and then pulled the gesture into a wave and held it there. Once the rain had filled her boots and chilled her body numb, she lowered her arm and stopped the recording. She uploaded it to her TikTok account and then replayed it as she walked inside, and again as she folded herself into bed. Under the covers she kept it running, watching herself stare into the kitchen as the man had done.

Very Private Little
Random Possibilities

—CHLOE WISE, 2021

Constantine was not cheating on Sabine. He wasn't cheating, but he regularly looked at photos of Emily Ratajkowski. He wasn't cheating, but he preferred to watch movies on his phone, alone. He wasn't cheating, but he turned away from Sabine if his towel dropped from his waist while he was walking from the shower to the bedroom. He wasn't cheating, but he'd bought Sabine an Apple Watch for her birthday. He wasn't cheating, but he left streaks of shit clinging to the porcelain bowl of the toilet for her to clean. He wasn't cheating, but he chugged drinks, gobbled food, cracked his toes, and bit his fingernails. He wasn't cheating, but these days he didn't stroke her hair and say how soft it was, no matter how carefully she washed and smoothed it out. He used to let fistfuls of it run through his hands. He used to ask to brush it.

And Sabine wasn't cheating on Constantine. She had never cheated on anyone. Not even in high school. Not even at art

school. Not even when she was cheated on in her early twen-
ties, although she was most tempted then. She didn't cheat
when a spray paint artist at a party gave her a nub of a conch
shell. Sabine never even once thought of cheating. Even when
men in hard hats whistled at her as she walked through the
city, and even when she wore a sundress to the local pool and
the horny mothers stared at her midsection as she tanned
herself on the concrete steps in the sun. Sabine didn't cheat!
Even when a very famous artist offered to paint her nude in
his studio, and even when Ruth introduced her to a man who
performed Bowen therapy. She didn't cheat when she was the
only woman at a six-week sculpture residency in Portugal, and
she didn't cheat with the lead singer from the vegan straight-
edge band even though he told her he would die if he couldn't
be inside her.

Sabine had cheated once. But she wouldn't do it again.

You Seemed to Me a Small Child Without Charm

—SAPPHO, 620 B.C.E.–550 B.C.E.

Mere hours after seeing the man in the garden, Sabine was woken by a need for painkillers. Her head ached and she had to squint with one eye to see the time on her phone. It was four thirty in the morning. She padded out of the bedroom and into the hallway and saw ahead of her, resting just inside the front door, a folded piece of paper. On top was her name, encircled by a heart.

> *It was so nice to see you, or should I say for you to see me. I loved it when your eyes connected to mine and your mouth made that big o shape. Did you know that when you run you actually lean the top half of your body forward, which is what professional runners do. I suspect someone has taught you how to run. You were faster than I thought you would be. I will say that you are a better runner than you are an*

*artist. Recently I have been following your career—
how lucky you are! So many awards. So much attention. Do you think it's fair?*

Sabine's heart went rat-a-tat-tat in her chest. She flipped
the letter over, and then back again, as if seeing it from all
sides would reveal something new. She read it once more, and
then not knowing what else to do, she slid it underneath the
front door and back into the night.

Skinned Rabbit

—ANTONIO LÓPEZ GARCÍA, 1972

Sabine woke again, midmorning, to her phone buzzing on the glass top of the bedside table. It rattled her tiny bottle of cannabidiol, a half-empty cup of valerian root tea, and a bulk pack of melatonin. She regretted the noisy tables and her incessant mess. In trying to answer her phone she managed to knock an empty soda can and a half-eaten apple to the floor. Constantine remained asleep, both hands folded across his face, blocking any light. Sabine was actively protecting her husband's peace. He had reminded her that not everything had to be brought to his attention. In fact, Constantine had insisted that she keep more from him. *I find independence attractive*, he had said. She was on the path to being an independent, peace-loving, peace-filled wife. She drew a giant letter *P* on his stomach, followed by an exclamation mark.

"Cecily?" said Sabine.

"We are less than a week away from your exhibition so

I've organised for the *Art + Fashion* interview to go ahead. I've given them your address and they'll be over there later this afternoon. There will be a stylist and a photographer, a journalist, and maybe some others."

The lead-up to Sabine's exhibitions left her for dead each time. Her art had its own ideas of what it wanted to be, and it shrugged off her plans for it like an insolent teenager. No one had warned Sabine that everything to do with exhibiting her work would feel like a lie. No one had told her that it would be the biggest shock of all when people lined up, walked in, and took her art seriously. As if it had been an intellectual choice to make such things. It was her opinion that as soon as she finished a piece of art, it morphed into something living. She felt no ownership over her exhibitions, only responsibility to keep them alive.

"I'm still a bit hazy on what *Fuck You, Help Me* is technically about," said Sabine.

"No, don't say that, you know very well what it is about," said Cecily. "It's about the struggle to exist alone and unencumbered in public at night. It's about threat and gender and all the roles we are forced to play. The work is *urgent*. The work is a *provocation*. The portraits are bleak but *utopian*, because—and this is a good point to make—you are using the city as a playground, while you are nude. What a dream. Let's pause for a moment to consider what an *impossible* dream that usually is for people who identify as women, non-binary, trans people and also, I guess, for some cis men."

"I've captured freedom, haven't I?" said Sabine.

"No, not freedom per se, but rather an alternative. A fantasy of reality."

"And the portraits are of me, but I'm a stand-in for all women and people and I also represent trans people and some men?" said Sabine.

"You're our mystical avatar. The bold, fearless sim. It's about *agency*, and *disobedience*," said Cecily.

"And you love it, don't you? You think it's good?" said Sabine. "That I'm being so unbelievably disruptive," she added.

"It is as intoxicating and transformative as licking the venom off the back of a Sonoran Desert toad. It makes me believe in art again. I couldn't sleep the first night I saw it, I was too energised. I rang my dear friend at midnight to tell her that I have this exhibition that absolutely fucks. I said, you got to see it, the thing is blinking, it's alive."

Sabine said goodbye to Cecily and got out of bed. She needed to be reminded of this amazing thing she had made. She rushed to her studio and opened the file on her computer containing her exhibition photos. She scrolled through them until they were a blur, then stopped and diligently clicked through each one.

"No," she said. She pressed the arrow key faster. "No, no, absolutely not, no."

Her exhibition would go viral. She was about to incur the public's praise of her disobedient work. She pulled open both wardrobe doors and put on a corduroy hat to ground herself, followed by one of Constantine's scarves. Art Basel might be next. The Venice Biennale. She added a bra and a coat, and her velour track pants. The Guggenheim was going to want her. A mid-career survey of all her puppets. She could hire actors to wear them, or acrobats, or other artists, or she could wear them and do a runway of each look. Sabine wandered barefoot into the kitchen. A stratospheric trajectory opened in front of her. She was ready, of course she was.

At the sink she drank half a Dr Pepper and ingested ten strawberries, several pretzels, and a container of yogurt. Still unsatisfied, she melted a knob of butter in a pan, then added half a cup of sugar. Once it became a thick caramel, she chopped in two ripe bananas and stirred until each piece of banana was coated in the warm brown caramel sauce. Sabine ate her bananas in her studio, haunted by the feeling of inevitable success. There was nothing to do except eat. Her luck had set its course and she was simply witnessing it.

Art + Fashion had featured all of Sabine's favourite living artists. Each issue wove photos and profiles together with acerbic interviews. She imagined the design team here, in her studio. She looked around the space. It heaved with bottles of glue and tins of paint. Scraped-clean pasta bowls and two wicker baskets of ribbons. A portable air conditioner. A carrot that was so old it had shrunk like a piece of withered seaweed. Sabine counted seven empty coffee cups. A dirty white feather stuck into a ball of tangled string. Several good pencils. Three cameras. An old phone. Two hammers and a bronze paperweight of a mink on its back. Wedged between the desk and the wall was a lid from a tub of hummus. A fly buzzed against the window, trying to escape.

With every intention of cleaning her studio, Sabine instead pulled another emergency packet of cigarettes from the top drawer of the filing cabinet. She opened the window, raised a cigarette to her mouth, and lit it, then puffed on it as though it was a cigar, letting ash dust the floorboards. A cigarette can be a meditation. A cigarette can be a Sunday service. Sabine closed her eyes and imagined the interview.

Hey, guys. Let me introduce myself. I'm Sabine, a thirty-eight-year-old conceptual artist. My personal style is playful, irreverent...

No.

Hi, beautiful people. My name is Sabine and I am a creative mongrel.

Worse.

Hello there. An average day for me usually begins with acknowledging the privilege of being a celebrated artist in this economy.

Stop.

Sabine relit her cigarette and searched for the interview section on the *Art + Fashion* website. Each profiled artist was photographed against the backdrop of their palatial studio. Even the messy studios, on a closer look, were curated maximalist spaces filled with art objects. The artists were shot in dominant, sombre poses. Their clothing was available to purchase by swiping up. One painter posed with an unused paintbrush and wearing a floral organza Oscar de la Renta gown. A sculptor holding a hammer and chisel wore seven-hundred-dollar reclaimed-denim jeans and a leather-panelled shirt. A writer sat, fingers poised above her laptop, legs crossed in eighteen-hundred-dollar boots. There was a lot to say about all this, and one day she would find the courage to be the person to do it.

She filtered the artists to see the ones like her, the conceptual creators. They wore acid-wash jeans and bleach-stained jumpers, vintage Air Jordan sneakers. No one could have anticipated the number of blunt fringes, and it was not an exaggeration to say that every single one of these artists clearly enjoyed cereal. No other studios were contained within a house. All of them were located in warehouses, in sprawling, high-ceilinged spaces. The artists seemed—and she double-checked to see if this was right—they seemed, yet again, unusually moneyed.

Sabine had only made a living wage in the last few years of her career. She spent the first year paying off her credit cards, which she had previously lived on, by using one to pay off the other and so on and so on. A babushka doll of debt. When she received her first large government grant to fund an exhibition that she had already made and was sitting in storage, the grant bypassed her pocket and went straight to the bank. She'd had four thousand dollars remaining but that quickly dissolved on a dental checkup, a subsequent root canal, a new computer, and a set of copper pots for Constantine. If she wanted to be honest, it had taken close to fifteen years for their combined income to arrive at the low six-figure range.

The sound of mechanical waterfalls interrupted her thoughts. Constantine's alarm. Constantine was triggered by the sight of her sitting and thinking. Preparation for his job included chopping, cleaning, and gutting. Thinking didn't count as work to him. Constantine opened the door without knocking. The only way you can derail an artist is via a lobotomy or by interfering with their thinking time. Art begins in the head. Barging in, making noise, even opening a door in another room, were all acts of violence. It was essentially a complete untethering. The nerve. Sabine's one good thought, of grinding harder than all the other moneyed artists, slipped through a cavernous crack in her mind.

"Would you interrupt a banker in an acquisitions meeting?" said Sabine. She exhaled smoke from her nostrils.

"I have some upsetting news," Constantine said.

"Would you slam the computer lid shut as a writer was

writing their booky little words?" said Sabine. She picked a shred of tobacco from her tongue.

She knew this would be the moment he chose to tell her he wouldn't be able to make her exhibition opening because of work.

"I need you there," she said.

"I will be there but maybe not exactly on time," said Constantine.

She scanned her body and found that somehow, in spite of the hurt, she was perfectly intact.

"Are you working today?" His eyes fell to an old, empty wineglass.

Sabine automatically lit another cigarette.

"I have a major interview," she said, as Constantine slid the ashtray closer to her. She narrowed her eyes and sat back in her chair, refusing to allow him to dictate where her ash went. It falls where it falls. Imagine thinking you could confine ash, the substance of the entire universe.

"Constantine, I fought for the opening to be on a Monday so you that you could come," said Sabine.

"Can you tell me again what time it starts?"

"I am forcing Cecily to open the entire gallery on a *Monday*! Do you know how rude that is of me?" said Sabine.

"But, my love, I just got this promotion," said Constantine.

Sabine let her arms drop by her sides and thumped her head down on the desk.

"I'll ask Ruth when it starts," he said.

Sabine remained slumped with her ear to the desk, continuing to smoke. After a moment, Constantine left. She returned to an upright position. He put the radio on in the kitchen and hummed along. Sabine kicked the door of her studio shut, the resentment building brick by heavy brick. Constantine put on a load of washing and took out the rubbish bins. She sat at her desk with her fingers on her temples. *Bastard.*

Sabine opened the studio door to tell him there was no way she was able to work through all the noise, but he was already gathering his keys, putting on his cap, and zipping his backpack closed.

"This exhibition is career-defining. I should be treated like a delicate egg in the nest of your warm love. Feather me. Give me your morning songs."

"Sabine, I've given you all my nests—in fact, I've made you a million nests—and I am now tired," said Constantine, walking towards her. He had fish to gut. The oyster man would arrive in forty-five minutes. He hadn't even made himself a coffee.

Sabine slammed her studio door closed. Opened it, then slammed it again, sat back in her chair, and waited for him to come and see what was wrong.

"Feather me!" Her yell was muffled from behind the door.

Sabine would be the first to tell anyone that she worked like a dog, head down, paws in the dirt. Breaking her wrists with effort. Sniffing. Digging. Puffing. She put meat on his plate. She put wine in his cup. Daily she engaged in very cool and sexy next-frontier thinking. She needed Constantine to be an ally, not another dog elbow-deep in the dirt. He was getting his dirt in her hole. *Stop digging!* His career trajectory was a hindrance to her own. It had all the hallmarks of the patriarchy.

"You are my wife," said Constantine, resting his head against the wood of the door. "You are my calm, understanding wife."

On the other side of the door, Sabine frowned.

"Do you want a hug?" said Constantine.

She threw a sack of prosthetic eyelids at the door.

Sabine leaned back and spun around in her desk chair. She would move to an art deco studio flat and date one of the young Italian waiters from his work. Stefano. Bruno. Both of them. She would sandwich herself between them every other day. Constantine knocked softly then squeezed the door open an inch.

"I love you," he said.

"Love you too," she said.

"I can see you're feeling annoyed," said Constantine.

"All the beautiful parts of your life are from me," said Sabine. "The flowers, the fridge full of your favourite foods, these beguiling gothic puppet skins. All me. Never forget how much beauty I bring in here."

Constantine raised his eyebrows. He glanced at a metal serving tray of almond-shaped artificial nails. With his foot he swept aside three plastic-wrapped bundles of human hair from Temu.

"Have you managed to get any sleep?" said Constantine.

"Do you believe in ghosts?" said Sabine.

"It's not that I don't believe in them, it's just that I have yet to see any evidence of them being real," said Constantine.

"They've been documented for centuries. There is an overwhelming amount of evidence of the spirit world," said Sabine. She picked at her thumbnail bed until it tore and bled.

"Half the time it's mental illness and the other half of the time it's old houses or the wind," said Constantine.

Her soulmate, the man she had chosen to be her legal family, then shrugged and retreated, leaving the conversation there.

He was unwilling to meet her in this moment, in her chaos, arms open wide. She regularly accepted *his* chaos, which arrived without warning. His menu planning. The half-day Italian sauces. She accepted that he left the floor littered with quartered onions and spilt stock. Even that he let the heater theatrically blow the discarded garlic husks in circles across the kitchen floor. Never in her life had she violently diced zucchini. Whereas he would stand there, hacking at those vegetables, the pieces of white and green flying over his shoulder, hitting her, *harassing her*, tumbling over her body and skidding across the tiles with the rest of his debris.

Sabine stood up with such force that she knocked her chair over. She charged down the hall after him and opened the front door so fast that the handle hit the wall. A sprinkling of plaster fell to the ground.

"Hey! I want to know how many waitresses you've slept with," said Sabine.

Constantine stopped walking and blinked rapidly at her. He glanced around. Mouth open. Mouth closed. His dinner plate hands hung either side of his Pooh Bear belly.

"Are you intermittent fasting again?" said Constantine.

"You said you would call in sick," said Sabine.

Constantine looked down at his checked pants and his clogs.

"I never said that," he said.

"But you could. People get sick," she said.

"Sabine . . ." he said, and as if that was enough, and as if she would know what he meant, he began walking away.

Someone on the street slammed a car boot closed with a whining clunk. Constantine stopped walking. He turned around.

"What did you say?" he said.

"It was a car door," said Sabine.

"You look really upset with me," said Constantine. "It's unfair to be upset at me for mishearing you."

"It wasn't even my voice."

"I work in a loud environment. My ears are dulled from it," he said.

Sabine was silent.

"I'm telling you this with love in my heart," said Constantine. "Sometimes your stress is like a nail bomb; it explodes and I have to absorb it all."

Sabine told Constantine that he was all bent under the weight of his own ego, and that only psychopaths start sentences with *The chef in me thinks*. Sabine accused Constantine of being godless and hypercritical, and said that he had an irrational desire to dominate every living thing he came into contact with, including their worm farm.

Constantine said, "And look, again I'm telling you this with love in my heart, but sometimes you behave like a mean, fussy, heinous—"

Sabine closed the door. She returned to her studio. She sat on the floor with her legs crossed and her head in her hands. After a moment she crawled over to the desk, lifted the empty glass down, and then tore a new bottle of wine from the carton under her desk. She clambered up from the floor to light another smoke.

Call it flayed. Call it attempted manslaughter. This week was trying to kill her in a spiritual sense. This week was mashing her along the floor of the underworld, with the Rembrandt Man, the oncoming interview, that husband. Propelled by stress, Sabine left the house without turning off the lights or heater. She headed towards the city. No jacket. No phone. She walked away from the house as if it had never been hers to begin with.

Now Muses, and My Genius, Help

—DANTE, 1314

It was midafternoon by the time Sabine returned from the shops carrying a bag containing an effortless pair of Christian Wijnants fringed trousers and Ann Demeulemeester Crinkle Nero boots. The sales assistant had agreed that the combination made Sabine look exactly like an artist. *A conceptual artist?* Sabine asked, and the sales assistant said, *Or an actual artist.*

As Sabine opened the gate to her house, her eyes fell to a piece of paper weighted to the front step by the doormat. She put down her bag and picked up the paper. Printed on it was a screenshot of her recent performance piece *Resting Beside Fast Cars*. For the installation, Sabine had dug a four-metre square hole beside the Mordialloc Freeway then sat in it wearing a gothic skin called *Perimenopausal*. The performance had something to do with the patriarchy, something to do with capitalism. The screenshot showed her posing with the shovel resting on one shoulder. On every visible piece of Sabine's skin someone had drawn onto the paper marks like bruises, like wounds. On her forehead was an oval drawn in red pen. Across her chest was a line. Another heavy line across her throat. She turned the sheet of paper over and read the words scrawled on the back. His writing, heavy handed and slanted vertically across the page, the letters becoming smaller and smaller.

> *I saw that you (yet again!) won another grant. The*
> *City of Melbourne gave you thousands of dollars—*
> *FOR WHAT? Are you choking on all the money you*
> *get given? I'm curious if you've ever made a piece of*
> *work and kept your clothes on? I saw a poster for*
> *your exhibition which is another piece of sexually*
> *provocative work. I have drawn a portrait of you. See?*
> *Anyone can be an artist. I assume you are a visual*
> *learner so pay careful attention—the lines indicate*
> *where your clothing should be. Sleeves. Collar. Hem.*

Sabine tensed. She held the piece of paper close to her face, her fingers shaking as she traced her eyes across each line the man had drawn. He had used a Biro against a ruler to draw line after line across each part of her body, dissecting her into pieces. A garbage truck turned into the street, whirring and crashing through the bins. Panting, Sabine hurried to unlock the front door, get inside. Her bones felt gelatinous. She flung her bags down the corridor towards the bedroom, then ran to her studio and shoved the piece of paper into a drawer of her desk and slammed it shut. She stalked to the kitchen and removed a butcher's knife from the block.

"Is anyone here?" she called. She wanted to look at the picture again. She wanted, if she were honest, never to stop looking at it. She held the knife in front of her with both hands as if it was a golf club.

"Hello?" she called.

Sabine stood in the doorway of each room. She opened cupboards. Got on all fours to look under the bed. She inspected the locks on the front and back doors until she was convinced they were useless. There were also the rotting windowpanes, the loose bolts. Glass, wood, brick—none of it was sufficient. She tried to call Constantine, but it went to voicemail. Ruth's phone, which she kept permanently silenced, rang out. Police? ACAB. The black handle of the knife became slippery with perspiration.

There was a polite knock at the front door. Sabine jumped.

"Yo!" someone called. "We're here for the shoot."

Another knock.

"Try calling her," a different voice said.

Someone pounded on the door with their fist.

In the bedroom, Sabine jumped into her new trousers and boots. She stood motionless, in her bra, and thought briefly of leaving it at that. She opened her side of the wardrobe to look for a shirt, running her eye over every piece of clothing hanging on the rail and in the drawers. None of them was representative of her in that moment. Pilled jumpers and faded denim. It was chi-chi! It was la-la! Sabine breathed heavily. She ran to Constantine's side of the wardrobe and dragged out the most expensive piece of clothing in the house, his three-piece suit. In the right light, on a good day, it would have been superb. On a bad day, it was both rumpled and too tight.

"I'm coming!" she yelled. She threw on the waistcoat.

Sabine raced to push all her silver rings onto her fingers at once. Three to a finger. She scrabbled to find her personal style. She took a waist bag from the door handle, put the butcher's knife inside it, and zippered it closed, then slung it diagonally across her chest. Undid it again and secured it around her waist.

Sabine answered the door, sweating.

The journalist, a photographer, and a stylist accompanied by eight bags and two boxes of camera gear stood on the step.

"So, you're the artist who makes the freaky dolls," said the journalist. He snapped on his Dictaphone and said, "*Dolls interview.*"

"I make gothic skins and self-portraits," said Sabine. She lowered her mouth to the Dictaphone and said, "*Multimedia and conceptual artist.*"

"Can you take us to the dolls?" said the photographer.

"Sure," said Sabine, "but my exhibition is really more a journey into a—"

"Let's see the little ladies," said the photographer.

Sabine stood aside as the design team shuffled into her studio.

The journalist spoke into the tiny microphone. "Sabine can't easily define her often tense and visually alarming work. She believes that her creativity flows from an unnameable space, which she described in a previous interview as being 'the deepest part of her psyche.' As one of the few internationally successful conceptual artists alive in Australia today, she is able to speak with authority on the process from beginning to end. One critic has labelled her 'insensitive and flippant,' while another proclaims her to be 'a driving force of brilliance. She is self-possessed and talented.' *Art + Fashion* is excited to sit down with Sabine and unpack her day leading up to her prominently advertised solo exhibition, *Fuck You, Help Me.*"

"Who was the critic?" said Sabine.

"Can you talk about the ethics around the use of live streaming in your performances?" said the journalist. "And would you call your approach to social media performative?"

He waited.

In their previous emails back and forth, Sabine had already mentioned twice that her performance art was experimental and that it often surprised her with its beauty and capacity to unnerve—*even in its seeming irrelevance,* she had confessed. Now, if she hadn't been so distracted by the letter, if she'd been able to find the words to say that live streaming was a way to coauthor a work with the public, if she'd had time to organise her thoughts, she would have said that the only true purpose of any art piece she made was to start a dialogue with the viewer, and that the quickest and most effective way to do that was in real time, online.

"Sorry, what was the question?" said Sabine.

"What's it like to be one of the headlining artists of the Goethe Gallery?" said the journalist. His energy demanded instant answers, and as she spoke he nodded in short bursts as if spurring her on.

"What project are you working on next?" said the journalist.

Sabine sat in silence. Words stopped in the mud of her mouth. All she could think of was the letter from the Rembrandt Man. It was as if she were swimming and a shark had bumped into her legs. How could she sit here and engage with the interview waiting for a bite to come? Her stomach clenched as the photographer set up a silver umbrella in one corner of her studio and placed a large foil disc on the floor.

"Let's get you sitting on a chair in the garden with a doll on your lap, ventriloquist style," the photographer said.

"They are wearable gothic body puppets," Sabine said. "What about if I stay inside and I just pose in interesting ways? I could do a backbend or stand on the bookshelf?" That would announce her avant-garde-ness to the public and keep her safe from the Rembrandt Man.

"Let's do the puppet first," said the photographer.

"Or another idea I had was to sit on my desk eating an orange. Casual and behind the scenes. End-of-the-day energy. An artist interrupted in the middle of unwinding..."

The journalist paced. "Sabine is robust, long-haired with bleached eyebrows. She is eccentric in the way that satisfies our expectations of successful artists. Her studio is dense with tools of the trade and lined with puppets, their mouths and eyes open and expectant. One window looks out onto an unruly garden. On the floor of her studio are several fallen objects, which, Sabine commented, 'sleep where they lie.' Sabine's space is a furnace of creativity; she's welcomed us onto the factory floor, so to speak, and sat comfortably to talk us through her average day. We kept up with Sabine through the frenzy of activity she maintains as a working artist."

Unceremoniously, and without seeking permission, the stylist cleared everything off Sabine's desk. Once it was bare, she arranged three pencils in a glass on one side, then gathered Sabine's journals, which covered the floor like fallen fruit, and stacked them. Her movements, the amount of cleaning and huffing around, all seemed judgmental. The stylist rearranged the ornaments. She put a plaster mould of Sabine's foot next to the old radio. A latex stomach from one of her puppets was balanced against a Glomesh purse. These things had no place being next to each other. Sabine watched as the stylist pulled her unmarked box of cowrie shells down from a shelf and rummaged through it.

"I think what I have learned about live streaming art is that people enjoy seeing things they feel they're not supposed to. There's a voyeuristic element to it that they like. It's never smooth or aesthetically pleasing, and I think that's the appeal for a lot of people," said Sabine. She cast the stylist a stern look.

The stylist unhooked the corkboard above Sabine's desk and put it face down on the floor. She pulled the curtains aside and opened the window. Sabine itched. The window needed to be locked closed. Her things needed to remain untouched.

"I'm having a tiny little, just a very small panic," said Sabine. She picked up her corkboard and hugged it to her chest, then sat in her swivel chair. The stylist pulled a mohair blanket from a bag and draped it across the back of Sabine's chair. She spent five minutes working on the purposeful creases, until the blanket was set in perfect waves. Then she touched Sabine on the shoulder.

"Your waistcoat needs steaming," she said.

"Is there any point if we rough it up in the shoot?" said Sabine. She spun around in her chair to face the stylist.

Sensing her tension, the journalist checked the Dictaphone was still on.

"I think we should really play to the absurd," said Sabine.

"Talk to us more about that," said the journalist.

"I think we need to make the whole shoot look really dramatic," said Sabine.

"And how is *Fuck You, Help Me* dramatic?" said the journalist.

Many ways. Sabine ran her hands through her hair and then plaited it. She was about to respond but became distracted by the open window.

"I'm cold, is anyone else cold? Shall we shut the window?" said Sabine.

The photographer slammed it closed without locking it.

"Where do your ideas come from?" said the journalist.

"I go through periods of gathering content for ideas and then I—"

"What about your drive to create?" said the journalist.

"I work to deadlines, so it's fear," said Sabine.

"Can you tell us an unusual fact about the upcoming exhibition?" said the journalist. "And what matters most to you?"

"That my art is meaningful, I guess," said Sabine.

"Do you have a funny story you can tell us relating to the puppets?" said the journalist.

The stylist did not love the crinkle boots, and instead Sabine was forced to stand barefoot in front of her shiny desk. Midway through the shoot, the photographer showed her some of the photos. Her studio seemed somehow grander than it was.

"You mentioned earlier that you enjoy making meaningful art," said the journalist. "In what way is your current exhibition meaningful?"

"Well, it's a fantasy that plays with power dynamics," said Sabine.

"Can you tell us about your studio?" he said.

"It's a humble space," said Sabine, looking up.

"In regard to fashion, what is your personal style?" said the journalist.

"Well," said Sabine.

"Drop your chin," said the photographer, "and look out the window for me."

Sabine sat on her desk, leaned forward with her elbows on her knees, and interlocked her fingers, then rested her head on her hands. She closed her eyes and smiled.

"Take off your bum bag," said the stylist.

"It stays on," said Sabine. She clutched the bag containing the knife.

"It's too bulky," said the stylist.

"I'm diabetic," said Sabine. "It's all my medication. I could literally die without it."

"Is this a rental?" said the journalist. He stamped his foot on the floor.

"I need you in an old jumper," said the stylist. "An oversized one with holes in it. It would look more flattering and also hide your special bag."

"What about if I get the orange, like I mentioned earlier, and I could peel it with my teeth or something interesting like that, and I can be looking at the camera but with my body angled away," said Sabine. She watched the journalist carefully, waiting for him to note how detail-focused she was. He remained silent.

"I've got oranges in the kitchen," said Sabine.

In the bedroom Sabine changed into a clay-brown fisherman's jumper. The design team were out of line not following her impulse with the orange. Everyone has seen an artist in a big jumper, but no one sees the artist having a snack in the garden, thinking about their work. People love to be taken behind the veil. Sabine resolved to fight for the orange and the intimacy it would create, but when she returned to her studio the design team were huddled around the camera, frowning.

"The light isn't great in here," said the photographer, "so we're going to move your desk into the living room and set it up there."

"But this is my studio," said Sabine.

"It will still be everything from your studio," said the journalist, "but better lit."

Feeling unbalanced, Sabine steadied herself by holding on to the back of her chair. As she did so, she brushed the stylist's carefully arranged mohair blanket onto the floor. Sabine made no move to pick it up.

Protect Me from What I Want

—JENNY HOLZER, 1982

Hours later, as the design team were leaving, Sabine found another letter, folded between the wrought-iron whorls of the garden gate.

> *Maybe no one has ever told you to act less of a whore. Sometimes you wear your robe with the flowers, other times, those small green shorts. Once I saw you in only a white towel. I like the shorts. Haha! I'm being rude, aren't I? You get it. You feel the need to wear them, so you get it.*

Sabine set her camera up on the tripod and stood in front of it. She live streamed herself with the intention of simply moving intuitively through her feelings. At first she threw the letter up in the air and let it float to the floor several times. Then she threw it and added a punch, hitting the paper with a grunt.

Finally, when she sensed the letter had received enough of her wrath, the idea came for her to scrunch up the beaten page until it was in the shape of a chrysanthemum, push it into her mouth, and chew. She left the live stream briefly to take out the other letter from her desk drawer, and when she returned she bit pieces from it like it was a sheet of seaweed. She sucked on the paper until it was reduced to soft bitter hairs across her tongue and then swallowed it, letting her membranes and muscles shove it deep into the wet dungeon of her body. Once those words were in the cage of her stomach, Sabine stopped the recording. It felt provocative. It also felt sensational. These letters were now art. Her ownership over them excited her. There was no need to check the comments. She had served the muse well.

She took off her jumper and threw it into the corner of the room. She slung the bag with the knife over her arm and rang Constantine. When he answered she didn't speak for a moment, letting the noise of his busy kitchen fill her ear. Pots banged. Something rattled. He yelled, *"Behind!"*

Sabine was conscious of the amount of space between her body and things. A few metres to the sofa. A generous distance to the front door. This house was too small for them as a couple, but too large when she was alone.

"Did you just see my live?" said Sabine.

"I'm at work," said Constantine.

"I have a stalker," said Sabine.

She undid her plait and shook out her hair. It was time to cut it.

"What?" said Constantine.

In the background of the call something sizzled and a woman's voice called out an order. Constantine yelled again. *"Hot!"*

"He wrote a letter saying he's going to physically attack

me." This was not an exaggeration, it was a fact she felt deep in her body.

"Who did?" said Constantine.

"The stalker," said Sabine.

Sabine walked to the bathroom, closing every curtain she passed. She opened the top drawer in the vanity and moved things aside. There were only a few places the scissors would be.

"Read me the letter," said Constantine.

"Can you come home?" said Sabine. She closed the drawer and opened the next one down.

"Send me a photo of it," said Constantine.

"He's obsessed with my work. It's creepy," said Sabine.

"I can't hear you," said Constantine.

She wished he would come home sooner; failing that, she wished he wouldn't deliberately stay back later. In the mirror she saw her face, wrinkled and sunken, and her lips pale and cracked.

"I'm being hunted," she said. Constantine was an island she was paddling towards, but the tide was taking her sideways.

"Did you go naked on TikTok again?" said Constantine.

"Excuse you," said Sabine.

"I'm not saying there's anything wrong with your art, this is not about blame," said Constantine.

"I could be killed," she said.

"Sabine, get the letters and read them to me," he said, but Sabine was in the mood to lock heads, nose to the ground and hooves in the dirt.

"I ate them," said Sabine. She wandered back through the living room and sank into the sofa. In the background of the call she heard something large and metallic clatter to the ground. Constantine swore.

"Don't eat things that are not food. I really can't talk right now. Can you go to Ruth's?" said Constantine.

"I need a personal alarm. One that notifies the police as soon as I press it," she said. Her belief that all cops were bastards had dissipated.

"Phoning them will be as fast," said Constantine.

"I need a big sound that will scare or deafen him," said Sabine.

"Use your voice," said Constantine.

"*Use my voice like this?*" she yelled. His ego, it was obscene.

"My love, I have to go. Text me," said Constantine. He hung up the phone.

Constantine sent her a message four minutes later. *Come to the restaurant. I will cook you a whole sea bass with new potatoes. Two bread baskets. Come and read a book and I'll dip in and out to see you when I can.*

Sabine wrote: *Can't. Going to Freya's exhibition.*

Constantine: *Great. I'll try and finish early and meet you there. Xx*

Something sharp scratched along the floorboards in the hallway. Sabine slowly stood up. The scratching travelled down the corridor towards the living room. She stared through the shadowy doorway into the hall. She held her breath. A croak. A series of clicks.

Sabine grabbed hold of the base of the chrome lamp. She unplugged it and wrapped the cord around the base, then took two steps towards the hallway.

A white bird as large as a child stepped through the doorway and into the living room. Sabine gripped the lamp. The bird kept one beady black eye on her as it raised its yellow beak to the ceiling and chattered. Sabine lifted the lamp above her head and ran at the creature.

So Shut Your Eyes
While Mother Sings

—EUGENE FIELD, 1889

The ghost of Carolee Schneemann swiftly heaved the albatross onto her hip to get the bird out of the way of the lamp's downward trajectory.

"Can you believe its wingspan is eight feet?" said Carolee.

She carried the bird into the room and sat down heavily on the sofa, the creature in her lap. Trying to still it, she stroked the albatross from the crown of its head all the way down to its flicking, feathery tail.

Sabine plugged her lamp back in. Carolee's edges fuzzed then sharpened.

"You look different from how I remember you," said Sabine. She leaned forward to study Carolee closely. Carolee had shrunk. She looked more compact, her dromedary hump pushing her head forward at an angle Sabine hadn't seen in a living being.

"It's not polite to comment on another person's appearance," said Carolee.

"Your eyes seem much farther apart than before," said Sabine.

Carolee stopped stroking the albatross. She lifted her hands to her forehead and slid it up until it lengthened, and her face narrowed.

"Better?" said Carolee.

"Um," said Sabine.

"Anyway, I came to tell you that he is standing outside that window, right now," said Carolee.

Sabine nearly leapt onto the coffee table. "Get me out of here. Levitate me away, we've got to leave."

"He loves being close to you," said Carolee.

"Which window," said Sabine.

"Don't move. Stop yelling. Sabine, be quiet and listen to me. Nothing good happens in the mind of a person who can stand as still as he is," said Carolee.

The ghost of Carolee Schneemann opened her mouth wide and a light shone out from her tonsils. From her mouth, a nature documentary was projected onto the curtain over the window. It showed the albatross, sitting on a ground nest and preening its feathers. Every few seconds the footage would warp and the clip would restart from the beginning.

"Those birds, right there, have no natural predators," said Carolee. "On an atoll in the South Atlantic they make ground nests and sit on their eggs. Then recently, I forget the intricacies of why, perhaps global warming, but the mainland mice got hungry and the sea levels retreated enough for them to run to the island, their feet wheeling wildly over the rocks, and when they reached the birds they barely broke their stride as they swarmed the nests and ate them alive." She turned to face Sabine. "And the birds didn't move an inch. Didn't fly away.

They sat there, apparently unaware they were being eaten by the hordes of mice that hung from their necks by their teeth."

"Can I pat the bird? I need something to calm down. I'm shaking, can you see? I can't hold my body still at all," said Sabine.

"Compose yourself," said Carolee.

"But I am the bird, right? That's what you're telling me," said Sabine.

"Actually, child, if you would listen to me at all, the man outside is the giant albatross," said Carolee. She pointed her finger at Sabine. "And you're going to be the swarm of mice."

"Can he hear us? Perhaps we should whisper," said Sabine.

"Where is your hunger?" said Carolee.

"Interesting question," said Sabine.

"Where is your bloodlust?" said Carolee.

"I don't like to think about violence," said Sabine.

"Why?" said Carolee.

"It's grotesque. It's distressing," said Sabine.

"But you make gothic skins," said Carolee. She gave the bird to Sabine, who unwillingly took it. As soon as Carolee left the room, Sabine put the bird on the floor and it toddled over to the potted monstera, turned in a circle once, and then sat.

Carolee's heavy footsteps hammered back down the hall. She kicked the door open wearing the skin of *Expectant Mother*. The skin featured a huge swollen belly and a plump, rosy face. Carolee had run into trouble pulling the mask over her head, and the face was now positioned so that she was looking out of the mouth hole. She squeezed each breast, squirting milk at Sabine.

"Stop! The milk is off," said Sabine. It was a mistake to fill those huge breasts with cow milk, only to be told, by Constantine no less, that human breasts don't make any milk until the child is born. As if it were common knowledge. As if being a woman would let her in on the intricacies of milky tits and so forth.

The bird stood up and chattered.

"Is this not thoroughly grotesque? It reeks. It's vaudeville," said Carolee.

"You're misusing her," said Sabine.

"This, my dear child, is nightmarish," said Carolee.

"Birthing bodies? The ripe firmness of a pregnant belly? These are all very fine, artistic, gorgeous things," said Sabine.

Carolee felt around the bottom of the belly, unzipped the stomach, and then stood with her hands on her hips, her feet apart in a wide stance.

"Be careful," said Sabine.

Carolee lifted her leg onto a chair, and a doll the size of a cat fell from the puppet, bounced, dangled, then swung from the short umbilical cord.

The albatross flapped in fright.

"You can pick him up now, he's scared," said Carolee.

"That's my only pregnant puppet," said Sabine.

"Anyone, and I mean anyone, who concocted this, this baby dangling here . . . What is dripping on my feet now? What am I feeling?" said Carolee.

"Amniotic fluid," said Sabine.

"Ugh," said Carolee.

"Seven hundred and fifty milliliters," said Sabine.

"Anyone who thinks it's gorgeous has a rabid spirit inside them," said Carolee.

"I don't see it that way," said Sabine.

"Just let in the idea that artists, through their very nature, are violent," said Carolee.

Reacquainted with My Limbs

—LULAMA WOLF, 2023

Later that night, only five days out from her own launch, Sabine stood in the middle of the crowd at Freya's highly anticipated sculpture exhibition, *(Im)Possible Offering: Reactivity & Justification.*

The sound of clinking glasses and the hum of voices filled the stark front gallery space. Cecily and Freya had converted a former church next to the old psychiatric asylum into one of the largest commercial galleries in the country. They had remodelled the area behind the pulpit, installing a bright red glass bar, and the pews had been repurposed into an installation in the foyer.

Although Freya was Cecily's partner, Sabine had dressed for Cecily's gaze, and hers alone. Keeping her hair glazed to one side was a clip covered with tiny candy-coloured pearls. She carried a minuscule faux-crocodile-skin handbag that fitted only her phone, one key, and a credit card. Ruth told Sabine she looked Parisian. Sabine told Ruth she was being stalked, and Ruth said she loved his nickname, understood it was terrifying, but also thought it was a kind of levelling up, career wise. She held Sabine by the ears and told her to focus on herself and on having fun, and to forget the fear of being stalked. Sabine agreed, then slammed two wines.

Freya's art practice had remained unchanged for the past twenty years. It consisted of everyday objects presented in farcical arrangements. One sculpture comprised four stacked bricks surrounded by a circle of clean sand. Another featured an erect metal drainpipe vomiting a satin pillowcase. When she looked at Freya's pillowcase, each rumpled line in the fabric rippled and rolled across the sculpture, gathering momentum as it cascaded over Sabine. Seven thousand dollars for a handful of river rocks in a commercial blender. Sabine squatted down next to the sculpture. It felt sentient. It was as if the blender was threatening her. As if it would turn itself on and send rocks hurtling across the gallery. This piece of art, if given a little taste of an electrical socket, would destroy her. *Remarkable.* Six thousand five hundred dollars for an inverted iron funnel supporting a lone green ostrich egg. *Precarious.* Sabine almost wept. *Divine.* The fragile egg sat on top of something whose whole function was designed to work. It was a symbol, Sabine was certain, of socialism. Or Marxism. A liquid modernity thing. Sabine accepted a third wine from Ruth with both hands.

Within half an hour she'd managed to step on someone's foot. "*Sorry,*" she kept saying, long after the person had moved away. Sabine continued her circumnavigation of the art but was ambushed by Cecily, who swept her into a hug. As they embraced, Sabine was softly caressed by the many layers of fabric that washed from Cecily's body to hers.

"You need to see this before I forget." Cecily rooted around in her bucket bag, feeling either side of her metal drink canister before pulling out a flyer for Sabine's show. It was an image of Sabine hanging from a wall near the highway overpass. *F*ck You, Help Me*, was printed across the top of the flyer in bold sans serif.

"The star?" said Sabine.

"It's an asterisk. Remember we went over this, there are rules in public advertising. We cannot advertise the word *fuck*."

For months they had gone back and forth about the styling of the title.

"I thought we agreed to style it with a *v* instead of a *u*. As in, *Fvck*," said Sabine.

"I'm sorry, no. *Fah-Vuck* is what I heard in my head when I read it like that," said Cecily.

"I am unhappy about the asterisk," said Sabine.

"Just focus on the overall tone of the flyer. Isn't it so unbelievably bleak and peak-industrial?" said Cecily.

"I thought we were going to use one of the images that Constantine took of me in the garden. You said the nudity would have to be censored otherwise," said Sabine.

"Those photos didn't work," said Cecily. "On any level. But see how we blurred your whole body out? It's just a kind of misty, grey area now." She grabbed Sabine by the shoulders and squeezed her. "But listen, not long until it's up on these walls. How do you feel?" Her tongue darted out as if ready to drink in the answer.

"Good," said Sabine.

"How so? Can you articulate it for me?" said Cecily.

"It's all very exhilarating." Sabine puffed out her cheeks and tossed her bag from one hand to the other. She stepped back, catching her voluminous sleeve on someone's vape and almost breaking the tiny bird bones of their art-loving body as she shook herself free.

"Apologies," she said.

"This is roughly the same number of people that we are expecting will be at your opening," Cecily said. "So mentally prepare for that."

"I'm not worried," said Sabine. She blinked slowly. On all levels except emotional she would be fine.

"So many artists disintegrate during the week of their show," said Cecily.

"Do they?" said Sabine.

"For some reason, even though it is a choice and a privilege, the whole process proves utterly destabilising for them," said Cecily. She raised her eyebrows towards Freya.

Freya approached Sabine, beaming. "Don't let all this intimidate you. I won't forgive myself if it puts you off."

Freya wore their usual Issey Miyake blacks and Air Max sneakers. From their left ear dangled one brutalist earring. "There's so much hype about *Help Me, Fuck You*," said Freya.

"She knows! Let's not freak her out," said Cecily.

"There's Samantha!" said Freya. "Samantha, over here, you've got to meet Sabine."

"This is the widowed collector I was telling you about," said Cecily, visibly excited.

Freya inhaled deeply. "She thinks your work is post-narrative."

"The highest compliment," said Cecily.

A woman in a friar's habit swished over.

"Sabine! I'm so delighted to finally meet you. Freya let me have a sneaky peek at the full digital catalog, and when I saw it I literally gasped," she said.

"It was audible," said Freya.

"It's unbelievably stimulating, isn't it?" said Cecily.

"There's a forgotten sensuality to the work," said Samantha. "Now, to me, your work actually functions as a sculpture, and I don't mean *sculptural*, I mean it's tangible, visceral, immobile."

"Thank you," said Sabine.

"And now that you're here in front of me, you must tell me about the *Fucking Help Me* process," said Samantha, staring at Sabine's mouth.

"You must," nodded Cecily.

Sabine tasted bile. The only way not to fall to pieces was to stay where she was, fists full of her taffeta dress.

"Tell Samantha the insight you had into duality," said Cecily.

"Well, it's a series of self-portraits while wearing portraits of myself," said Sabine. She let go of her dress, lifted her hands to waist height, and circled them through the air.

"The mind boggles. What's the story behind that?" said Samantha.

"It's about pretending to be something you already are," said Sabine. She reversed the initial direction of her hands.

"Or is it about risk?" said Cecily.

"Or is it about being perceived as something only partially true? You're demonstrating there is a permanent falsity to the selfhood," said Freya.

"It's about the face and the body and the night," said Sabine.

"*Of course* it is," said Samantha.

Sabine excused herself. She hurried to the bathroom where she locked the door and opened her bag, looking for crumbs of codeine, or Endone. Something. Anything. What if when the widow saw the full exhibition she thought it wasn't interesting? Or, even worse, what if she thought it was interesting but executed poorly? Sabine checked her phone to see if Constantine had messaged, but there was nothing from him. *Where was her husband?* She sent him several question marks.

The truth was, Sabine was on her knees for art. She prostrated herself before the altar of art. She spent her whole life in the process of making or recovering from art, and when she wasn't doing either of those two things she was looking at other people's art. Art bubbled her blood. Art sliced her open and let the universe pour in. As soon as she passed through the doors of a gallery, or a studio, or even when she opened a book on art history, she felt it fill her. That deep, anticipatory whomping worship. Sabine was reorganised in the presence of great art. Her atoms shuffled and resettled.

Sabine closed the lid of the toilet and sat on it. She held her phone up and went live on TikTok.

"Hey, just wanting to come on here and discuss Freya's sculptures," whispered Sabine. "They are such spooky, obsessive artefacts. Majestic tokens. The concept that Freya's art is right this moment being sold to collectors, who will lock it away privately, disturbs me. Like, money enforces a separation between the artist and their creation. Do you think it's a crime that Freya's reinterpretations are only available for one person? Shouldn't it be a more prolonged public experience? Let me know your opinions in the comments."

Motorised_Cooter commented: *Once I was high on mushrooms & idk if it was a gallery or an aquarium or what, but as*

soon as I walked in, the walls turned into oceanic portals to another dimension, and so I sprinted out of there so weird

JahBlessSelassie commented: *Artists are the new mystics*

Ruthsexycool commented: *Are you in the bathroom? Come
out, I'm bored*

BiPolarBear commented: *Artists are the new art*

"Okay. Interesting comment. As an artist I'm wary of the
pressure to market myself instead of my art," said Sabine. She
touched her ears, smoothed her hair, checked her clip.

MorrisseysFirstWife commented: *Off topic but are you
wearing a nine hundred dollar dress in a recession?*

Ruthsexycool commented: *Let me in I'm at the door. I'm literally banging*

BiPolarBear commented: *Pookie is in her luteal phase*

Ruthsexycool commented: *The wine is running out*

Sabine stared at her screen. Only fifty people. As she waited
for more to join, the number dropped to forty-one.

"Oh, sorry, I think I have to go," said Sabine. She stopped
the live stream.

Sabine emerged from the bathroom and she and Ruth re-
joined the crowd. They stood through the second hollow acknowledgement of country by a benefactor of the gallery, who
beamed into the audience like a proud parent, their hands
shaking as they held notes typed in oversized font. After a
smattering of applause from the room, Cecily adjusted the microphone and called her lover's art profound. Freya thanked
everyone for coming, lifted both hands to the ceiling in a vic-
torious pose, and claimed that every piece had sold. Sabine
raised her glass and committed fully to the chronic and debili-
tating contractions of jealousy. Ruth whistled loudly. Everyone
clapped. Someone somewhere dropped a champagne flute to

the polished concrete floor, where it shattered in a shimmering smash.

Sabine found herself stumbling backwards through the crowd, her body propelled away from Freya's successful exhibition. She didn't mean to turn around suddenly and edge people out of her way, but when that didn't work she transitioned into ploughing through them like a barge on a river, not so much pushing people as guiding them out of the way like rubber ducks.

"Coming through," she muttered.

Behind her, Ruth and Freya were remonstrating with the DJ, who had mistakenly stepped on the ring of clean sand around the bricks. The DJ took to the decks in outrage and played grime far too loudly for the space.

As Sabine approached the exit, she preemptively took a breath, preparing to hunker down and bulldoze through the last of the crowd, but Constantine was at the door, waving to her.

"Go back," she mouthed at him. She walked into the tasselled edge of someone's scarf and inhaled a loud haze of musk perfume.

Wheezing, she made her way over to him. "I can't do it. It's too much. Can we go?"

"You want to leave? You told me it was essential that I come. That my presence would make you feel safe and you could enjoy yourself properly. I left work early and stopped by the house to shower first. I thought it would be nice for us to have some fun together at the after-party—" Constantine peered over her shoulder. "Just ten minutes?"

"My art is terrible." Sabine burst into tears.

"Is it?" said Constantine.

Sabine let Constantine steer her out through the double
doors of the gallery. They stood in the street. He held his jacket
above her head to protect her from the light rain and she grate-
fully leaned into him, letting him take her weight. A marriage
can be scaffolding. It can be a vehicle to leave in.

He told her that her photographs were too weird to be boring, and too well done not to demand serious attention. "*Am I
right?*" he kept saying.

"*I guess so,*" she replied.

"I think I age twenty years in the week leading up to your
showings," he said.

"Imagine what it's like for me," said Sabine.

"It all gets very intense. The air in the house. All of it. Everything," he said.

Perhaps it was strange to see the spectre of creativity rid-
ing your spouse like a jockey. Sabine wanted to understand
more of his experience of her. She let go of Constantine for
a moment while she buttoned her coat and then caught his
hand again, desperately, and he allowed himself to be grabbed
like this, and she wanted to thank him for the acts of grace he
gave her time and time again.

"Are you sure you don't want to go to Freya's after-party?"
said Constantine, hopefully.

"God no," said Sabine.

"I'll dance with you," said Constantine.

"I'm too tired," said Sabine.

"How was Ruth?" said Constantine.

"Good, but can you imagine dating someone ten years
younger? Lou is twenty-eight," said Sabine.

"Sure," said Constantine.

As they turned into their street, Sabine slowed her pace.

She came to a stop at the mouth of the alleyway closest to their house.

"Can we try something?" She took hold of one of his hands and drew him into the alley until they were both hidden in darkness.

"What are you doing?" he said.

She faltered. "Reconnecting."

A car passed, casting them in a spotlight for a moment, and she saw how tired Constantine was.

"I want to make extended eye contact with you," said Sabine.

"Okay," he said. He took a step closer so that they could see each other's faces in the dark.

"It's a technique for deep connection and intimacy," said Sabine.

Constantine remained openly gazing at her.

The eye contact became too much for her after a few seconds. Sabine looked away and told him that they were good for each other. Constantine agreed. She told him that divorce would never be an option for them, not in a million years, not after all of this. Constantine replied by saying that he wasn't aware she'd ever considered it.

"That's all I needed," she said.

He exhaled quickly and gave her a very small, quick smile.

"Do you want to keep going?" she asked.

"Let's go home," he said.

Constantine walked ahead of her. At the house, he used his forearm to stop the gate slamming into her, his key already in his hand.

Constantine fumbled with his keys, scraping them over the door lock, unable to find the entry point in the dark. He dropped the keys, and as he reached to pick them up he held on to the door handle, which twisted open.

"You didn't lock the door?" said Sabine.

"Of course I did," said Constantine.

"It's open," said Sabine.

"That lock is faulty," said Constantine.

"No, it isn't," said Sabine.

"We're going to have to get it looked at," said Constantine. He walked straight into the bedroom. Sabine hesitated. She raked her thoughts clean of paranoia, refusing to glance down the hall in case someone was there, waiting. She walked into the bedroom, normally. She took her earrings off and her clip out, normally. But she couldn't quite stop herself from standing in front of the window and staring at the back of the curtain. She imagined, briefly, the Rembrandt Man staring back.

Constantine undressed quietly and crawled into bed.

"Should we try it again now?" she asked. She would do it for him. If it would help them to feel close. She could make herself maintain the contact, and feel his vulnerability, and not be frightened by it.

"Please, can you just..." Constantine turned away and shrank into a ball.

"Can I just what?" said Sabine.

"Hold me?" said Constantine.

He took her hand and kissed it and placed her hand over his chest, which she squeezed, remaining careful not to hurt him with her nails.

"What did you love most about our wedding day?" said Sabine.

"Well, you wore your yellow thing with the puffy sleeves, and those huge blue flowers," said Constantine, sleepily.

"Turquoise delphiniums," said Sabine. "And you wore the silver smoking jacket and matador pants I found for you."

"That's right. And my vow was to let you be you," he said, "which I do, and which you are, very much."

"And mine was to put our love first," said Sabine.

Sabine kept reminiscing aloud, in as much detail as possible, only pausing to check he was still awake. The more she spoke the less she would think about that unlocked door. She reminded Constantine about the mint-flavoured narwhal-shaped cheese-cake that Ruth made, and he let her polish the memories until they were smooth. *I've been wrong*, Sabine thought. *Marriage is constant movement between two people. A kinetic thing.* She had caught up to Constantine and lost sight of him again within the space of a day. Awash with blankets, they deconstructed their love until it was no more a mystery to her than glowworms or comets.

Sabine moulded her body to her husband's, even pushing the tops of her feet into the soles of his. She hugged his body tightly to her own. She wasn't sure what more to say to him.

"Thank you," said Constantine.

Trouble Moving On?

—ISSY WOOD, 2021

Later, when Constantine's breathing slowed, and his skin seemed to glow with that radiating sleep-heat, she kissed the back of her sleeping husband's head and waited. When he didn't stir, she lifted her arm from his chest, slipped out of bed, and left the bedroom.

Sabine began the checks that had, in a matter of days, become her new routine. She slid her hand under the bottom of the curtains to feel whether each window was locked. She checked that the back door was locked by unlocking it and then paying careful attention as she drew the iron bolt back into the doorframe. The sound of metal sliding into metal had become a chime, a bell, a very good sound. The sound, Sabine thought, was worth the feeling of terror that came from unlocking the door in the first place.

Sabine ensured the linen closet and pantry were empty. Looking into the bathroom, she unhooked each towel from the back of the door and let it fall to the tiles so that she knew, visually, that those dark shapes hanging were not people. No Rembrandt Man here either. However, looking behind one door meant that all doors needed to be looked behind. She began at the front of the house, tiptoeing, swinging each door closed and open again as if airing the room out. Taking mild comfort from knowing, even if only momentarily, that the house was still hers.

But as soon as she finished her rounds the need to check resurfaced. The feeling nagged at her until, like an animatronic thing, she caved in to the compulsion and checked all the spaces again, sometimes a third, fourth, fifth time. It was wise to always assume he was there. It was safer to expect him, because it removed any element of surprise.

With another round complete, she felt listless. Should she pour one out? She might as well. She pulled a glass from the back of the kitchen cupboard. Trapped in the thick lip of the glass were tiny bubbles of air. The glass was solid; she'd once seen Constantine wrap it in a plastic bag and pound a chicken breast flat with it. The house waited for her to resume checking as she filled the weapon with whisky and kept pouring, letting it overflow onto the kitchen bench. She sipped, trying to ignore the thought telling her to check the cupboards under the benchtops. She imagined the Rembrandt Man crouching behind the cupboard door, waiting for her.

Sabine stepped back and took hold of a cupboard handle. If he was in there she would kick him, run to the front of the house, and wake Constantine and they would fight him together. She braced herself, turned one foot to point in the direction she would run, and bent her knee ready to kick.

The cupboard was full of copper pots and pans. No black-clad wide-eyed men.

Her breathing was ragged as she went into the laundry, her perspiring feet slipping on the tiles.

"Enough," she said. She pulled her phone out of her waist-band and booked an Uber, using the other hand to rummage through the laundry hamper for something to wear. She dressed in a musty black turtleneck and some Adidas snap pants, then tiptoed back along the hall, past the bedroom. She stopped. She listened. Was he pretending to sleep? The snores had lost their natural timbre. Sabine double backed to the bedroom, trying to recall the rhythm of his usual snores. She crept into the room and over to the bed. She leaned over her husband. One of his eyelids fluttered.

"Are you pretending to sleep?" said Sabine.

A rich, mucus-laden snore vibrated through him.

She crouched on all fours next to him and stared at his face, his chest. She picked up his hand and dropped it, to test.

Sabine crawled around to her side of the bed and picked out a dollar coin from the pile. She crawled back to Constantine and placed it in the centre of his chest, facing it tail side up to the ceiling. If he was really sleeping, she told herself, the coin would still be there when she got back.

At the front door, she held her phone close, tracking the cartoonish icon of a car as it slid down the streets of the map until it was directly in line with the house. When she heard the Uber beep, Sabine sprinted to the car.

I Should Not Allow Anyone
to Inconvenience Me

—EMILY BRONTË, 1847

It was midnight when Sabine arrived to see Ruth and Lou arguing in the rain. Behind them, noise from the underground after-party leaked into the otherwise empty street. Sabine was unsure whether she felt buzzed because of her own stale dregs of adrenaline or the night's lawless energy.

"I'm going to leave if you don't drop it," said Lou. "Like, I will seriously leave, and you will never see me again."

Ruth stumbled backwards. "I'm asking you to explain why that dusty girl in the ruff was touching your arm."

"Hi," said Sabine.

"Hey," said Lou, "good to see you."

"Likewise," said Sabine.

Ruth stamped one Cuban heel into the pavement.

"Lexi is an incredible artist and a good friend," said Lou.

"In what sense?" said Ruth.

"She's attractive. She's gorgeous. Sexiness exudes from her

whole being, and we had a thing *ages* ago, so it's out of both our systems and you can relax," said Lou.

"She's in there with those milk-saucer eyes, probably high on one pill stretched four ways between her and her cargo pant–wearing friends," said Ruth.

"I'm so disappointed by your jealousy," said Lou.

"Why don't you ask Lizzy to reread your thesis every time you make one little—" said Ruth.

"Her name's Lexi," said Lou.

"That's right, and she *quilts*," said Ruth.

Lou sucked his vape. "The tapestries of her internal and external diaspora are more evocative than your whale cakes." He tucked his vape in his pocket and descended the stairs to the bar.

Ruth hissed at Lou's back.

"Do not go in there, they're awful," she said to Sabine.

"It's really not good for me to be at home right now," said Sabine.

"Okay, me too," said Ruth.

"You crossed me off earlier," she said as she dragged Sabine past the security guard with the guest list.

At the bottom of the stairs was a metal table with prefilled glasses of prosecco and small bamboo bowls of bruschetta topped with marinated roasted vegetables. Sabine plucked two glasses of prosecco from the flock, sipping from one and then the other. Holding the acidic liquid in her dry mouth until all her teeth were wet again.

"Do you think he's going to break in?" said Sabine.

"Who?" said Ruth.

"The Rembrandt Man," said Sabine.

"I doubt it," said Ruth.

"Do you think we should move to a new house?" said Sabine.

"Constantine would never," said Ruth.

"Should I move out, then?" said Sabine.

"No point. I passed four posters of you today near Parliament Station. He'll be able to find you through the gallery, and you're online all the time," said Ruth.

The muggy basement bar was shaped like a train carriage, long and low-ceilinged, lopsided with the narrow bar on one side and the crowd on the other. The after-party heaved with industry people, jostling together like cattle. Sabine placed her open palm in the middle of strangers' backs as touch points as she picked her way through the crowd.

At the bar they finished their drinks and then ordered martinis so cold that flecks of broken ice swirled through the chilled liquid. Anchored to the bottom of each were meaty olives as big as quail eggs skewered onto wooden cocktail sticks. An olive bulged in Sabine's cheek as she chewed.

The drinks were weak; she wouldn't say it aloud, but they were watery. She reached a hand up her shirt and unclasped her bra. The urge to scream came and went.

"We should mingle, but I cannot be bothered," said Ruth. She stepped in front of Sabine, shielding her from two well-known grey-haired sneaker-clad art journalists.

"Everyone here has an insatiable appetite for art, every single one of them, except us. Let's do the rounds then get ramen. You can stay at my house tonight," said Ruth.

"As long as we do something," said Sabine.

"All these fucking artists need to get a fucking life." Ruth brushed past a woman with a shaved head wearing a necklace with the word *KETAMINE*.

Sabine nodded hello to the woman but ignored plenty

of others. People recognised Sabine from the saturation of marketing for her exhibition. Once they had recognised her, though, they ignored her, an entirely Australian response to the perception that she had received too much attention already. She had felt more warmth from her community before she was successful.

"Stay here, I'm going to the bathroom," said Ruth. She dropped Sabine's hand and disappeared through a swing door.

A man texting knocked into her, apologised, and then held her by the hips to steady her. The pleather of his jacket and his woollen hat wet from the rain had a damp-dog smell that was now so high up her nose that it may as well have been in her brain. The man said sorry again, his hands burning into her hips. She was stuck, pinned by people. Her Rembrandt Man could easily have followed her from her house. She scanned the crowd, looking for a malevolent face. By coming here, Sabine had stuck her legs through some Regency chop frills and lain down on a plate for him to eat her. This party was a plate. This city and her house. Sabine backed away until she was at the far end of the bar. She stood mutely on the periphery, unable to penetrate the swamp of bodies around her, expelled so far back that her heels touched the wall.

Looking down, she saw that near her right foot was a slug trailing a hectic path of mucus. The soft-bodied mollusc was only inches from dozens of pulping sneakers and pounding heels. Sabine put her arms out to stop people from walking too close. She pushed someone in the chest.

This was a proud slug, its head upright and alert. As Sabine bent down to look at the creature more closely, the slug reared its glistening head back to look at her. It rippled forward, its tentacles desperate for grass. Sabine patted her pockets for a tissue to serve as a makeshift platform to place her slug on. The slug put its head down. Inched closer then stopped, its tiny, boneless body unable to travel the distance between them.

"Don't you worry," said Sabine.

She reached for the creature, but as soon as she touched it, the slug stiffened, flopped, and rolled.

"Try to relax," she said.

Sabine gently rolled the slug into the palm of one hand. She placed her other hand over the top, making a cave. She could feel it moving. A constant, tiny tickle.

"Lou's talking to the ruff again. Should I intervene?" said Ruth, sidling up to Sabine.

Sabine turned to Ruth. "You will never guess what I have."

She briefly lifted her hand to show Ruth the slug.

"Are you saving it?" said Ruth.

"Obviously," said Sabine.

"Just get another one, you can eat as many as you like," said Ruth.

"What?" said Sabine.

"I'll get you more," said Ruth.

Sabine stared at her friend.

"No thank you," said Sabine.

Ruth shrugged and then ploughed through the crowd towards the metal table laden with bruschetta. She quickly returned with two bowls. One bowl had grilled zucchini bruschetta and the other was covered in thick strips of marinated eggplant.

"Jesus Christ," said Sabine.

She lifted her hand to her nose and sniffed. *Garlic?* She

angled her hand towards the light. It shone. *Oil?* Sabine, searching for proof of her own sanity, brought the slug to her mouth and licked it.

"Do you want ramen?" said Ruth.

Sabine lowered her hand. "I think I need to go home."

A Cosmic Awakening

—SUCHITRA MATTAI, 2023

The storm lowered its head and charged along, unmooring screen doors and slamming them closed with irregular claps. Paperbark trees bowed down. Roosting birds raised their hackles, and possums clung by their claws to bucking branches, weathering each gust of wind. Electrical wires bounced and swished between telegraph poles, while grit and leaves and empty takeaway containers slid across the road with a grainy rattle.

The house, alert, noticed Sabine arrive home and walk straight to the bedroom, her keys clanging in her hand. In one motion she retrieved the coin which sat on Constantine's chest like an anvil, slightly left of centre, but tail side up to the ceiling. The house sank farther into the crumbling blocks of her splintered foundation. Weeds curled through the gaps in her weatherboard hem. The stumps of her feet cold, damp, and muddy. Her roof rusted open in flaky holes. The wood of her walls croaking as it swelled and shrank. The house shuddered in the storm winds, her windows loose in their panes. The house endured Sabine as she roamed, ricocheting through each room like a gallstone. Sabine was constantly awake, pacing from one end of the house to the other. *Sleep.*

The house let her back door break loose and swing from one hinge. She warmed the woodworm larvae until they prepared to erupt. Legions of termites nibbled. The steel diaphragm of the house bent, fracturing thick pieces of wood. Mould bloomed across her ceilings in silvery spores.

Sabine remained awake, wandering from room to room, checking again that the windows were locked and placing her ear to each door. Checking, always checking. Her cold fingers shocking the house with each touch, as if the storm and the mess weren't enough. *Sleep.*

When It Became Apparent
That Both Men and Beasts Were
Wearing Themselves Out
to No Purpose

—LIVY, 59 B.C.E–17 C.E.

The next morning, Constantine was mid-piss when Sabine swung the back door open by one hinge and spotted him standing in the sunshine. In her hand was a bowl of scraps that she had chopped into even smaller bits for the worms to eat. She paused, waiting to see if Constantine would notice her.

His face was tilted up as if he was looking at the sky, but his eyes were closed. He was a picture of serenity. Chin up, cock out. He bent his legs and swayed back, letting the last of the golden arc of urine splatter onto the base of the lemon tree. Hips pressed forward, he pulsed slightly on the spot.

Here, watching Constantine laying his heavy piss into the grateful dirt beneath the canopy of lemons, Sabine saw her husband's soul-fire. Cheeky. Dynamic. *What else?* He was self-contained. He was so perfectly unbothered.

Sabine pulled her phone from her back pocket, lifted it to frame him, and took a photo, but the shutter sound betrayed

her. Constantine's eyes flew open. He twisted away from her
and tucked himself back into his pants in one motion.

"You scared me," he said. He scowled as he re-buckled his
belt, and then hurried past his wife into the kitchen.

"Sorry," said Sabine. "I'll delete it."

In Search of the Miraculous

—BAS JAN ADER, 1975

Rigour, Sabine wrote. It was the beginning of her artist statement. She lifted her pen from the paper and held it at eye level to admire the gold ink. This pen was about to tear through the space-time continuum to exhume the meaning of her exhibition. This pen would reveal her process—oh, let this pen convey what her art was all about. Sabine pointed the glittering tip at the page and closed her eyes. She prepared to receive the glinting words that were about to pour down her arms like fresh milk.

Sabine opened her eyes. She underlined the word *Rigour*, then circled it.

Sabine put down her pen and flexed her fingers. She opened her laptop and launched a new document. She placed her fingers onto the keyboard, as focused as a concert pianist.

Rigour, she typed. The space bar pulsed. After a while, the screen darkened.

In the kitchen, Sabine drank iron tonic, warm Coca-Cola, beer. She stepped around the overflowing bin, which was surrounded by a smattering of coffee grounds and broccoli stalks, wasted unless fed to her worms. The pomegranates on the dining table were now the colour of mulberry and tobacco, and had shrunk in the sunlight until they were no longer baubles but cubes. Their leather skins gripped the rotting fruit inside, taut stomachs on display. Sabine ignored the dripping tap over the sink. She inspected each of the apples. Most were browning and soft. Some had turned to juice in the bowl. Sabine chose the firmest apple, took one bite, then rested it on the bench near the sink, turning it slightly to the side until the sunlight hit its waxy green skin.

Sabine found Constantine's recipe for bombe Alaska. She established, twice, that they didn't have all of the ingredients, but nonetheless she took out a carton of eggs, cracked two into a clean bowl, then wandered off. *Constantine*, thought Sabine, *would have no trouble telling me about his menu.* The process, the muse, clearly inhabited everyone else. Sabine clenched her jaw. It took her half an hour to make her way back to the studio and her laptop. Pillows needed fluffing. Lamps needed dusting. One spider commanded her full attention for a few minutes straight. "Such a beautiful web," Sabine said, over and over. "Whatcha want to catch up there in ya beautiful little home?"

Her chair beckoned.

At her desk, committed once more to the idea of work, Sabine picked up the pen. The artist statement bloomed in her gut. It was coming. Her art was about to be given a backstory. She braced for it.

Rigour.

Sabine was no more an artist than a monkey was a slice of ham. The effort it had taken to create *Fuck You, Help Me* would pale before the horror of people asking her to say something interesting about it. That Sabine was an artist should be the least interesting thing about her art, but here she was having to cram the vast silken mass of her exhibition into plain words.

An urge to vacuum came over her. Sabine pushed the Dyson from room to room. The performance of vacuuming; or, the performance of domesticity, the dance of procrastination. Sabine was in the foreground of each room, being art. She took the nozzle off and dragged the raucous, sucking tube along the skirting boards, eradicating dead skin, dead flies. Task completed, Sabine stamped on the button, rewinding the cord back into the machine, and as it zipped along, she acknowledged that *rigour* was not the right word.

"Come to me," she said aloud.

Sabine circled her hips, summoning the muse. She needed the spectre of creativity to appear. She wanted to open her eyes and see it wearing its velveteen suit, its tar-black hair like melted wax. The spectre was a doppelgänger for Nick Cave, and if the spectre of creativity insisted they touch, hip to slender hip, she would consent. Gothic, slinky, ridden in musk and opium; Sabine imagined the spectre of creativity's unwavering gaze flowing over her. Her face flushed and her infant heart cried in her chest. There was an illegal amount of abandonment sliding through her veins. Where was her muse?

Sabine sat on the edge of the bathtub, scrubbing the soles of her feet with a pumice stone until they were bright red. She showered, lathered, and rinsed her entire body twice, and then got out and rubbed coconut oil all over herself. She took as much time as she needed to perform the act of pressing something into her skin. She hitched each leg up onto the vanity to rub the oil in large circles down her shins, her calves, and all over her long feet. Once she was fully greased, she put on underwear and an old shirt of Constantine's, as well as a pair of his mountaineering socks, and then lay on the bed and waited.

Glorify Me!

—VLADIMIR MAYAKOVSKY, 1916

At noon, Sabine heard the next letter slip under the front door. In the hallway, she stood over it. She placed one foot on top of the paper briefly, before picking it up and reading it.

> *Clearly you want me to take control well ok I will! I could open the window right now—imagine!—and I could drag you by your hair from the bed. Do you want this? I think you must. You would love it (I would too).*

Sabine, in a panic, called Ruth, who told her to get out of the goddamn house. She pulled on one more pair of underwear and the tightest jeans she owned, like armour. She tucked a knife into her bag, balled her hands into fists, then swung open the front door.

The Girl and the Goat

—CECILY BROWN, 2013–14

If Sabine's house was on the northern side of the city, Ruth's apartment was dead west. It was near the smelting works in the industrial area. Sabine sat in the back of the Uber watching TikTok, flicking from one clip to the next every time there was space for a panicked thought to materialise. She washed out her brain with the internet.

As soon as Sabine arrived, Ruth ordered them some food. She told Sabine that she would look after her. Sabine told Ruth not to worry, because she wasn't going to cry. Ruth asked why she would say something like that. Sabine shook her head and told her again not to worry. Ruth cried because she thought Sabine was being unnecessarily stoic. Sabine cried at Ruth's ability to be instantly empathetic. Sabine said that having a stalker was overwhelming, and Ruth stopped crying.

"Write your own letter," Ruth said. "Write out everything,

like he's doing. Override his letters with your own. Make the story yours."

"Reinterpret?" said Sabine.

"Hijack," said Ruth.

"I think I'm being haunted," said Sabine.

"Every artist I admire, every single one of them, is haunted," said Ruth.

"Who?" said Sabine.

"I can't think of their names now," said Ruth.

"Are you?" said Sabine.

"Nothing has come for me yet, but I'm waiting," said Ruth.

Their lunch was delivered and they sat at Ruth's Formica table and unpacked takeaway containers from two paper bags. Sabine cracked open two small tubs and pinched edamame and folded shredded seaweed into her mouth. Ruth opened the sashimi and tempura prawns. She stabbed a prawn with a chopstick then ate it quickly.

Ruth interspersed mouthfuls with jokes and memories.

As she ate, Sabine live streamed herself. She knew she was actively inviting complete strangers—perhaps even the Rembrandt Man—to look at her through a screen. *The difference is the intention*, she thought. *The difference is that I am in control.* Sabine propped her phone against the bags of food and faced the camera towards herself.

The purpose of the live stream was to boost publicity for the exhibition. *It makes me so happy every time you go live*, Cecily had texted after one of Sabine's more voyeuristic streams.

There was a shared vulnerability between her and her followers. She was revealing her interior world to them; equally, they were vulnerable enough to show their interest in it. Her viewers loved to see her performing the most mundane tasks. Pulling weeds. Scrubbing the shower screen. The more domestic, the better. Whenever she went live during chores or while eating, people joined and, surprisingly, stayed.

"Are you live streaming me?" said Ruth, thumping the end of a large bottle of sriracha.

"Just chat normally," said Sabine.

"Well, I'm really worried about you," said Ruth.

"Let's talk about art," said Sabine.

They each poured out their knowledge on the current state of the art world and picked over the details together. They were careful not to blame anyone, and the Goethe wasn't mentioned, nor were arts degrees, commission rates, or pay discrepancies. They didn't even name any artists who got assistants to make work for them. Sabine told Ruth that artists had to fight very hard not to be changed by gallery representation, they had to make sure they stayed true to their original vision. Ruth said that artists should be given a living wage and left alone. That the best art she ever made was at a residency in Iceland where she was fed three times a day and talking was prohibited. Sabine told Ruth about how, in ancient times, artists were revered as much as priests or wizards. Ruth said that, in a parallel universe, they would be treated as rarified beings. *Gorgeous idea*, they both agreed. *Interesting concept.*

PoetryHag commented: *That lunch is worth more than my life*

Y2KNostalgia commented: *This is too podcast-ish. Do something else*

AliBabaFashionSlutzz commented: *Eat louder. Give us mukbang*

Sabine put down her chopsticks and pulled out a container of noodles from a bag.

Gyal_with_the_Gyat commented: *Sabine you are my favourite artist would I be able to email you something*

EarthAngela commented: *Not good art*

Sabine slumped back in her chair, ignoring everything except the last comment. She turned her live stream off.

"What happened?" said Ruth.

"Someone was mean," said Sabine.

Sabine clicked on EarthAngela's profile. She friended her. She messaged her: *Elaborate.*

Sabine could see that EarthAngela was a middle-aged woman who dabbled in ceramics and lived in a nearby neighbourhood with her smiling, happy family. Sabine found her Instagram easily and friended her husband and both daughters. She clicked on the eldest daughter's profile and looked at pictures of her twenty-first birthday. She liked one where the girl was posed with one leg crossed over the other in front of a purple balloon arch. Their Staffy had recently beaten cancer. EarthAngela's husband had taken up marathon running and lost ten kilos.

Sabine copied the daughter's name into Google and, through LinkedIn, saw that she was a five-star-rated real estate agent. Sabine gave her one star.

Sabine messaged the daughter: *Your mother doesn't have a single clue about art.*

Sabine returned to EarthAngela's profile. She reported every photo of EarthAngela's ceramic wares as possible terrorist activity.

"What are you doing?" said Ruth, squinting at Sabine's phone screen.

"I'm being bullied by a ceramicist," said Sabine. She quickly reported three more photos.

"Okay, enough," said Ruth. She took Sabine's phone and placed it face down on the table. Ruth embraced Sabine, and let her bend her neck like a tired swan and rest it on Ruth's shoulder. She reminded her she was loved marrow-deep. When Sabine reached for her phone, Ruth slid it farther away and told her, *"relax, relax, relax."*

Why It Is That Women Are Chiefly Addicted to Evil Superstitions

—JACOB SPRENGER and HEINRICH KRAMER, 1486

Later that afternoon, after watching a fair few episodes of *The Nanny* and half a documentary on eyewitness accounts of mermaids, Sabine left to meet her fate. Above a mechanic's grease-stained workshop, in an open space with crash pads and a boxing ring, a mixed martial artist called Carlos taught Sabine women's self-defence. It was a three-hour introductory course. The studio smelled of stale sweat and rubber, and on the walls were enlarged photos of Carlos, with black eyes and bleeding lips, being awarded golden championship belts. Apart from Carlos and Sabine, the only other person in the gym was a muscular young Asian man, skipping rope.

"The changerooms are next to the protein display," said Carlos.

"I'm wearing this," said Sabine. She looked down over her tight jeans, feeling the compression of two sets of underwear.

She lifted one knee and tried to pull it towards her chest, which triggered heartburn.

"You'll be fine unless you've eaten recently," said Carlos.

"Empty as a drum," said Sabine.

For the first hour, Carlos made her practise saying, "No," and, "Stop." He encouraged Sabine to yell, "Get out!" He told her that the goal was always to disarm and unbalance her attacker. Carlos said that if her Rembrandt Man came through the door waving a baseball bat, the best thing to do was to hug him. "He can't swing his arms back and you're now so close to his body he's lost his power of force."

"What is power of force?" said Sabine.

"This," said Carlos. He pushed Sabine in the shoulder, and she fell to the floor.

Carlos said that if her Rembrandt Man grabbed her from behind, one way to break his hold was to imagine her butt was an anchor, and to drop it to the floor.

"Basically, if you sit down, you'll be hard to carry," said Carlos.

"And then what?" said Sabine.

"Run somewhere safe, somewhere with lights and people, or the middle of the road. Hide if you find a good spot, but otherwise bolt as fast and for as long as you can," said Carlos.

"What if he chases me?" said Sabine, standing back up.

"I mean, he will for a bit. If he thinks he can get you he'll keep going."

"And then what?" said Sabine.

"Depends," said Carlos.

"What if he tackles me to the ground?" said Sabine.

"There's a move. You hook their feet and roll, and sometimes it works, but if you stand up and he's still on the ground, he's probably going to grab your foot like this." Carlos dropped to the floor, clasped his hands around Sabine's foot, and pulled her over. She fell to her knees and slid along the mat on all fours, her body dragging against the plastic ground with a loud squeak.

"I hate this," said Sabine.

"This is good stuff to learn," said Carlos.

"I think I'm having a panic attack," said Sabine.

"I'm going to tell you what I say to the teen girls I teach. You should see them, they're fifty-odd kilos wringing wet. They are a wafer to a man who wants to do something bad, you know what I'm saying? So, I tell these girls, you are weaker, that's a fact, and you are also smaller—that's another fact—but here's the kicker: no one, and I mean no one, is more vicious mentally than you lot are. You can cancel me if you want, but women are absolute psychos."

"Have you seen any statistics on what happens to stalking victims?" said Sabine.

"No," said Carlos.

On a short drinks break, Carlos chugged from a bottle of honeycomb whey protein and then burped.

"Let's go over what I told you earlier," said Carlos.

"The softest parts to attack are the groin area, the inside of the foot, his nose, his eyes, and the upper stomach," repeated Sabine.

"Now tell me what you're going to do to each part," said Carlos.

"Destroy it," said Sabine.

"Let's stick to the script. Instep?" said Carlos.

"I use the heel of my foot to stomp it," said Sabine.

"Solar plexus?"

"Punch it as hard as I can, which will cause shortness of breath or cardiac arrest," said Sabine.

"Only if . . ." said Carlos.

"Only if I can maintain balance while doing it," said Sabine.

"The floor is lava. You do not want to end up on the floor," said Carlos.

"The floor is lava," echoed Sabine.

"His nose?" said Carlos.

"Break it with the heel of my hand, strike up aiming for a spot behind his head," said Sabine.

"Noses are fun because they explode. I always tell my students to prepare to get blood on you. Remember, you're not punching the surface of his body, you are aiming to punch *through* him," said Carlos.

"Beyond him," said Sabine.

"Eyes?" said Carlos.

"Dig them out of his head," said Sabine.

"And how will you do that?" said Carlos.

"Thumbs," said Sabine. She flicked her thumbs back and forth like Carlos had showed her.

"Okay, we're getting there. What about groin?" said Carlos.

"Knee it, grab it, kick it," said Sabine.

"I'm going to tell you something else for free," Carlos said. "Just from watching you, I can tell you're giving it a good go, but you're uncoordinated. The best thing you can do in a combat situation is to be unpredictable. So fight, scream, dance, spit, go nuts—okay? Repeat back to me what I said."

"I need to be unpredictable," said Sabine.

"It's the only thing on your side," said Carlos.

Throughout the lesson his phone glowed with incoming phone calls from his fiancée. On his lock screen was a picture of her with an abundance of eyelashes and a ponytail longer than Sabine's leg. Clearly proud, Carlos held up his phone to give Sabine a better look.

"She's gorgeous," said Sabine.

"She knows all these techniques too," he said. "I would never let her leave the house otherwise."

Before the course finished, Carlos ran drills where Sabine repeatedly punched the torso of a rubber mannequin.

"How tall is the bloke?" said Carlos.

"Like you," said Sabine.

"Six-one, then," said Carlos. "Practise palm heel strikes to the throat and the nose. You're not just aiming to break the bone of his nose, you're really wanting to drive the bones up into his skull."

When Sabine caught sight of herself in the gym mirror, she was wide-eyed and pale. Carlos stood beside her, correcting her technique. Sabine saw the face of her Rembrandt Man in the mannequin's. She punched the Rembrandt Man in the throat and then grabbed its head and twisted as if trying to unscrew it from the neck. A guttural sound escaped her. She kicked the mannequin and then kneed it in the crotch. Sabine dragged her nails across its face and howled.

"That's the way," said Carlos.

With the Last Vibrations
of Her Jangled Nerves

—GUSTAVE FLAUBERT, 1857

Thursday night. Four days out from her exhibition. Sabine sat in an armchair in her living room, exhausted from learning to defend herself. She rested her legs on the footstool, opposite the ghost of Carolee Schneemann, who lounged on the sofa. The living room was heaving with snakes, each of them with a slightly differently shaped head. Carolee wore pedal pushers and a pair of orthopaedic sandals, and on her lap was a bronze snake curled into a knot. A multitude of earth-toned serpents slithered from one piece of furniture to the next. They were under the curtains on the north-facing window, on the kitchen countertop, curled around the bin. All she saw were tails and heads entering or exiting behind something else. The whole house smelled like piss and mice and hay.

"This is not my snake, but I assume it can untangle itself," said Carolee.

"Do you ever cage them?" Sabine asked.

"What would be the point? They're fine like this," said Carolee.

"Is the one in your lap aggressive?" said Sabine.

"I wouldn't know, it doesn't speak to me," said Carolee.

"Why are there so many?" said Sabine. In the kitchen, a snake travelled along a shelf, its tail slapping across the top of each of the mixing bowls as it went.

"I love the waves of their body and how muscular they are. You can go to a bodybuilding gym and not see muscles like this," said Carolee. She pointed out different breeds around the room. "Double-headed python. Zebra jungle jag. Nitty-bug zorbit."

"I can, in a way, see the appeal. Their sinewy bodies, et cetera," said Sabine.

Carolee held the bronze snake tenderly, turning it from side to side, admiring it. The snake lengthened itself out, then flicked its tongue, tasting its environment.

"This snake wants a little pinky," said Carolee.

"Don't feed it here," said Sabine.

"He's saying, 'Let me eat a frozen mouse, Mummy,'" said Carolee.

"Don't," said Sabine.

"I promise you, there'll be no mess," said Carolee.

"Are you cold? Why is the heating off?" said Sabine.

"Do you know about Nure-onna? It's a Japanese legend, a woman with the body of a snake and a normal human head. She kills people but she's very, very clever. She carries a small bundle with her that looks like a baby, to lure people closer to her so she can eat them. Like I said, she's clever, but she's also sad. Sometimes this can be a terrible mix in a woman. Anyway, when their environment is this cold, I am warm, so they snuggle close to me." Carolee lifted her shirt to show two snakes curled into her abdomen.

"You'll take them all with you when you go, won't you?" said Sabine.

"Pretty much," said Carolee.

"I can't stop thinking about the Rembrandt Man," said Sabine.

"And he can't stop thinking about you," said Carolee.

"I keep thinking about him breaking in, and what he might do once he is inside," said Sabine.

"That's not entirely true, though, is it?" Carolee tossed the snake aside and sat forward.

"I think about it constantly," said Sabine.

"Lies," said Carolee.

"What?" said Sabine.

"Tell me what you're really scared of," said Carolee.

"I'm scared of what he wants to do to me," said Sabine.

"Stop lying," said Carolee.

"It's anti-feminist of you to deny my feelings about this," said Sabine.

"I'm telling you to look, actually look, at your feelings. What is the feeling you're calling scared?" said Carolee.

"I'm itchy and hot, and I can't focus my eyes, and I have zinging energy in my legs, and my chest aches like it has been packed full of things, and I need to yell and—"

"That's called fury," said Carolee.

Fever Dreams

—LAUREL NAKADATE, 2009

There was a world, or a time, where Sabine and her husband, and her Rembrandt Man, frolicked together in sunlit meadows carpeted with daisies and clover. Wearing white linen and feeding each other crisp green grapes, *hey nonny nonny*. There was a time, surely, when they canoed together as hippies under a starry sky. They paddled through reeds and rushes, looking at the nighttime canopy of trees that hung in intervals along the bank. Sabine could hear the sound of their oars lapping at the lake, she could smell each of their patchouli-laden Afghan coats. Perhaps they huddled together, the three of them, in the canoe, as hippies do, though where they were going, Sabine couldn't say.

Sabine reimagined them as siblings, friends. A mother and two children—Constantine the mother, she and the Rembrandt Man as jealous toddlers. Sabine adored the variation in which they were band members, fighting over their fee at a regional pub. She was pissed off at both of them for overplaying, each of them insisting on multiple solos, and afterward, in the green room, she used her electric guitar like a sword and struck them with it, comically at first, but then seriously.

But her favourite variation, the tessellation of dynamics she returned to time and time again in her daydream, was the one in which she walked two loyal Dobermans on leads, their black coats shining, their faces those of her husband and the Rembrandt Man. Regularly, the dogs strained against their leashes, but Sabine jerked them back to walk alongside her. A helix of devotion, and intimacy, and control. Let's get back to them on a leash. Let's get back to them with ears pricked for her command. Her dogs, her loyal, obedient, needy dogs. Noses in their metal bowls, scoffing down food she made for them. Chasing balls and sticks she had thrown for their entertainment. They didn't want to be around any other dogs, or any other people. Even with those bounding long legs, they were unable to jump the fence of her control. Every effort to escape failed and they remained permanently enclosed. They remained her dogs.

Your Love Touches Me, but I Can't Return It, That's All

—ANTON CHEKHOV, 1895

On Friday morning, Sabine wore a silk robe, which billowed out behind her as she paced with the Bialetti in one hand and her mug of coffee in the other. As the toilet flushed, she took a step forward, then stood stock-still facing the bathroom door. Constantine jumped when he opened it. She held his eye.

"Are you hungry?" said Sabine.

"A little," said Constantine.

"Are we close at the moment? Like two rows of teeth in a shark's mouth?" Sabine pointed at herself, "First set," then pointed at Constantine, "second set."

"Sabine, I—" said Constantine.

"I want Frida and Diego shit. Yoko and George shit," said Sabine.

"Yoko and John?" said Constantine.

"I want to be a translucent kangaroo joey in the pouch. Am I in your skin pocket?" said Sabine.

"I am late almost every day. You start these conversations when I'm halfway out the door," said Constantine.

"I need you," said Sabine.

"Can we please take things down a notch. It's not even ten," said Constantine.

"I want you to want to smell my skin," said Sabine.

"Now?" said Constantine.

Constantine gathered his wife into his arms and gently stroked one of her eyebrows. He loved her big eyes and complimented them regularly, and she often responded by saying that blue eyes were a sign of inbreeding. Constantine would insist she didn't look inbred at all.

Sabine swatted away his hand. On the other side of the city, Constantine would gut sea life with the same hand that wore his gold wedding band. Those big hands. Those chopping, yanking, scalding hands.

"Stay home with me? Have breakfast with me?" said Sabine. She took his hand and dragged him down the hallway to the kitchen.

The thing was, Sabine had cooked Constantine one hard-boiled egg, and it sat there, steaming, on a floral-patterned saucer next to the sink. Sabine had watched that egg bounce and bobble in the boiling water for eight minutes straight. She'd even silenced her timer so that Constantine wouldn't get the hint that she was surprising him with an egg this morning.

"Uovo," said Sabine, letting the Italian word roll out of her mouth.

The egg on the saucer was an icon of love. There was something so unbelievably tactile about the surface of the creamy shell, and the way it rested atop that sweet ceramic dish. Hand-painted? She removed the egg briefly to check—yes.

Constantine put on his cap, and then clattered around in the pot cupboard until he found his travel mug. He took the Bialetti from her hand and poured in the remainder of the coffee. He opened the fridge door and pulled out a carton of oat milk and added a splash.

"The fridge needs a big cleanout. We've got lamb in there that's already a week old," he said.

She waited for him to notice her egg. She cleared the dishes from the bench, stacking them one by one on top of each other in the sink. While scraping a pan into the open bin, two fat flies emerged from the rubbish, buzzing and knocking into each other. Sabine used her fist to punch the waste down into the bin until the lid was able to close.

"It's important we nourish ourselves," said Sabine.

"Do you know where the umbrella is?" said Constantine.

It had been a great idea to make the egg for him. It would fill his belly and give him sustenance for the long morning ahead.

"The green-lipped mussels are coming today," said Constantine. "We've got a function, so I'll be home late."

"How late?" said Sabine.

"Okay, I'm off. I love you." He raced out of the kitchen, plucking as he went one browning apple from the fruit bowl.

Sabine stood in the middle of the kitchen and watched him trot all the way down the hall to the front door, slip his clogs on, then leave without looking back.

No Fear of Depths

—PATRICIA PICCININI, 2019

The radio in the print shop blasted classical music loudly across the cobbled laneway. The smell of warm ink and chemicals reminded Sabine of the overworked photocopier from art school, which ran hot and heaved dramatically through each print job as if it would be its last.

Although this shop produced high-quality fine art and photography prints, the place itself was void of any aesthetic effort. Yellowed Perspex screens separated each of the monstrous machines, which chirped and whirred like large-scale battery hens. Clumps of warm grey dust clouds rested on most surfaces, while layers of guillotined paper strips lay discarded on the floor. Two men worked the shop, barking out job numbers and answering the ringing phone with their infamous staccato welcome. A father and son, Sabine assumed.

Each of the photographs for her exhibition was printed on thick matte paper the length and width of a suitcase.

The colours were rich and deep. Most of the photos she had selected depicted her hinged at the waist, booting the night air in front of her. They were action shots. Her body swung through the air, and her knotty hair streaked out behind her. If anyone called them narcissistic, she would have a hard time proving they weren't.

Her eyes glazed over as she inspected the prints. Sabine leaned closer, squinting to see every detail. They were perfect. The flighty chaos of her nightscapes were better than she thought they could be. The streaky defiance of her nude body, the arresting features of her puppet skins rattled her loose from her worries. It was good work.

"These are divine," Sabine said.

"I'm glad you're happy with how they turned out," said the man.

"They are daring and provocative and they have this thumping power behind them, don't they?" said Sabine.

The son walked over, looked at the prints, and said nothing.

"The costumes are very unnerving," the older man said.

"The nudity is pretty front and centre," the son said.

Sabine swallowed. "They're utterly amazing," she said.

"Glad you think so," said the older man. He folded her receipt in half and ran his finger along the crease.

The father wrapped the prints as if they were cold children, jacketing each one in two delicate pieces of paper. Sabine waited patiently while he lifted and wrapped her work with deliberate care. He used his forearms as a forklift to transport the prints from one bench to the other. Walking at a slow pace so that the paper wouldn't bend in a way that would cause damage.

Outside the shop, Sabine cradled her package. When the

Uber arrived, she sat her collection next to her on the back seat. Each time the driver cornered, she gripped onto her artworks to stop them sliding along the seat and hitting the inside of the car door.

They entered the four-lane street towards her road. The outer ring of northern suburbs raced by, grey and beige and grey by turns. Her package threatened to slide across the seat again, but Sabine clutched it, holding it safe against the upholstery.

Prodigal Self

—EARTHEATER, 2019

Fuck You, Help Me #1
Sabine naked within a gothic skin, *Waitress*, clinging to the
edge of a sea cliff

Fuck You, Help Me #2
Sabine naked within a gothic skin, *Siren*, hanging, one-handed,
from the edge of the Edinburgh Gardens pergola

Fuck You, Help Me #3
Sabine naked within a gothic skin, *Maenad*, swinging from a
highway overpass

Fuck You, Help Me #4
Sabine naked within a gothic skin, *Venus*, hanging from a sub-
urban fence

Fuck You, Help Me #5
Sabine naked within a gothic skin, *Baby*, swinging from the dilapidated roof of a Californian bungalow

Fuck You, Help Me #6
Sabine naked within a gothic skin, *Crone*, hanging from a closed taco truck

Fuck You, Help Me #7
Sabine naked within a gothic skin, *Kali*, clinging to outdoor gym equipment

Fuck You, Help Me #8
Sabine naked within a gothic skin, *Baba Yaga*, hanging from a horse's saddle

Fuck You, Help Me #9
Sabine naked within a gothic skin, *Mystic*, hanging from the second tier of the Hochgurtel Fountain

Fuck You, Help Me #10
Sabine naked within a gothic skin, *Stay at Home Mother*, clinging to the Goethe Gallery front door security grille

Fuck You, Help Me #11
Sabine naked within a gothic skin, *Athena*, swinging from a rusted drainpipe

Fuck You, Help Me #12
Sabine naked within a gothic skin, *Hecate*, swinging from the overhead handles on a tram

Fuck You, Help Me #13
Sabine naked within a gothic skin, *Lilith*, hanging from a residential share house balcony

Fuck You, Help Me #14
Sabine naked within a gothic skin, *Gaia*, hanging from the back fence of the Standard Hotel

Fuck You, Help Me #15
Sabine naked within a gothic skin, *Persephone*, mid-drop from a eucalyptus tree

Worship Me, seven-minute film
Materials: animal blood, acrylic resin.

For Five Minutes I Considered
Myself Utterly Disgraced Forever

—FYODOR DOSTOEVSKY, 1871–72

On Friday afternoon, the large and airy exhibition space at the back of the Goethe Gallery was empty apart from a ladder on wheels and four rolls of duct tape. Sabine placed her bundle of photos onto the floor and slid her feet out of her Crocs, then walked around the gallery space, running her hand along the bare wall. Caffeine and adrenaline mixed like a strange soup inside her. The top of each femur ground into its corresponding socket, two mortars in two pestles.

"What if this is my magnum opus?" Sabine asked Boris, the bump-in coordinator, each time he walked anywhere near her.

Cecily pushed the door open with her shoulder while steadily eating salad from a Tupperware container. Snuffling at her heels was Feather, her old sable papillon with unfortunate ears.

"The tote bags are incredible," said Cecily. "We preemptively ordered truckloads."

"I'm certain this is my magnum opus," said Sabine.

"Art is all there is, right, Boris?" said Cecily.

Feather ran in circles, barking.

Boris shrugged as he tore a strip of tape off a roll with his teeth. "There was a time when I would have agreed," he said, pulling up his jeans, two sizes too large for him.

"Feather, shut up," said Cecily. She stabbed her fork into the container, hitting a cube of cheese and a miniature disc of cucumber.

"I think we should start with the title on the south wall and then hang the photographs chronologically from left to right, or alternatively we can be boring and hang them numerically as per the list," said Cecily.

"No, no, no," said Sabine.

"You said you wouldn't mind if I threw my two cents in—" said Cecily.

"No, I said I would mind," said Sabine.

"So what's the plan?" said Cecily.

"I propose we hang each picture based on the leg positions," said Sabine.

"Have you written the instructions down? How will we know this magical leg order?" said Cecily.

"I will know it, once I see them up," said Sabine.

"You want Boris to spend his afternoon hanging them, only for you to rearrange them?" said Cecily.

Boris stopped walking to look at Sabine.

"Why else would I be here?" said Sabine.

Freya hurried in, their torso crowded with tote bags. They draped the bags in a pile by the door.

"I was just saying to Sabine the exhibition is going to be

amazing, especially when it is hung chronologically, which makes the most sense," said Cecily.

"If you look at each portrait, I'm kicking. So it's the kicks that are the indicator of order. I would rather lie down and die than hang a portrait featuring a right-angle kick next to one with two flaccid legs," said Sabine.

"I can see both working," said Freya.

"And I am seeing all parts of myself fan out like a Balinese dancer's arms. Every part needs the exhibition to look a certain way," Sabine announced. It was unethical to hand the reins to the gallerist last-minute.

"Put it in your artist statement," said Cecily, "which I'm still waiting for."

Feather jumped up and down, ran in another quick loop, then collapsed onto Cecily's left foot.

"I see what you're saying. The legs are like arrows, pointing the viewer in the direction you want them to take," said Freya.

"This exhibition is backed by the second most expensive marketing campaign the Goethe has ever run. You've signed a contract that says I have the final say, so," Cecily clapped her hands twice, "let's hang it chronologically."

"It's a visual story of legs," said Sabine.

"What I'm hearing you say is that you are experiencing the common phenomenon of *hyper control*," said Freya.

Cecily turned to Sabine. "I am advising you—it's all about the swinging-naked, skin-wearing, gothic-what-have-you woman, and it only makes sense if the night gently darkens *chronologically* in the background of each photograph."

"Be more experimental," said Sabine.

"Be less self-sabotaging," said Cecily.

Freya mimed punching the wall softly. "Yes to what Cecily said, but also I am in no position to comment as I experienced a life-changing auditory hallucination during the lead-up to my exhibition. In the middle of my studio, a piece of aeriated concrete said to me, not with its mouth but with its energy, *Don't ever do another fucking group show,* and I won't. I was tempted at the time but my little brick didn't want me to do that. You've got to trust what your art is telling you."

Cecily aggressively speared a radish. "Hell is an artist three days before their exhibition opens."

Sabine left, striding across the gallery and storming through the foyer. No one followed her. She stood impatiently waiting as the double glass doors to the street shuddered open. *It was a story of legs!* Cecily was forcing her art into the box of chronological time, which frankly didn't even exist. Sabine squeezed through the slowly widening gap, smacking her arm into one door as she left, the force sending the glass pane into an irretrievable wobble.

Energised, she walked home, not moving aside for anyone else. She whacked the top of a letter box. Slapped fences. Kicked a parking meter. Cecily didn't understand she was her own work. Her art was her. She was the entire exhibition, the product and the manufacturer. She was the visionary that lived inside this magnum fucking opus. She was the boat *and* the sea! The sky and its many clouds! Brown donkey/green mountain. Grandfather sun/grandmother moon. In fact, since seeing her exhibition printed, the force of her wild and miraculous work had hit Sabine so fully, so utterly completely, that it had become impossible for her to believe she was anything less than a young god.

R U Dumb?

—JME, 2011

When Sabine arrived home, pink-cheeked and sweating, she found flyers for her exhibition had been shoved into their bronze letter slot until it was choked open.

Sabine's first feeling was not fear. Without checking behind her, she unlocked the door and swung it open, sweeping the flyers on the other side of the door out of her way. She entered the house, deliberately stepping on the pile of paper, the images crinkling under her boots. She twisted her feet, purposefully tearing some.

She closed the door behind her, locking only the deadbolt, and left the mess as it was. Bending down, kneeling, scurrying around on her hands and knees to clean up would have felt like performing an act of service that he had requested. She didn't even look to see if there was a letter. She ignored his offering completely.

What Sabine did do was notice the afternoon light, and when it streamed through the parted curtains and into the house it was golden.

She Was Terrified, and,
Astonished, She Recoiled
from Herself

—OVID, 8 C.E.

Sabine spent Friday evening alone in her studio. She placed a knife on the table in front of her and stared at it. It was an object made to slash and slice and cut. It wanted to do these things in the same way a mask wants to be worn or an axe yearns to be swung through the air. Weapons were not dormant; they were only ever waiting for willing hands.

"Get out of here," Sabine said under her breath. She tried again, louder this time. "Get your filthy hands off me."

She reached under her desk to pull a fresh bottle of wine out of the torn cardboard case. She lit an emergency dart, kicked the door to the hallway closed, then gripped the edge of the desk.

Sabine wanted to be a six-foot-tall man. A seven-foot monster. She shook the desk. She wanted to be at the top of the food chain. She finished her cigarette, opened her laptop, and slapped the play button on Best Rap [fire emoji] Playlist To Break The Aux [fire emoji]. Picking up the knife in one hand, she imagined what it would be like to grasp her own cock in the other. She wanted to twang her erection until it flicked back and forth between her hips. Sabine held the knife up in an ice pick hold. She swung it through the air. She thought of what it would be like to hump the dick into foods and pillows. Sabine wanted to bang her exhibition silly; was this possible? If she could borrow a dick, an idea of a dick, surely her exhibition was allowed to borrow a body. She imagined her exhibition on its knees, choking on her pink until spit streamed out the sides of the exhibition's mouth. She was in up to the exhibition's lungs, plunging in and out, penetrating creativity and success. She gripped the edge of the table again and closed her eyes. She was amazing! Who thought like this? People with dicks! Sabine sipped her wine. She was liquifying and re-forming as a petrol-fuelled engine. Sabine looked down at her lap. Was it her cock she was imagining or the spectre of creativity's cock? Sabine barely stopped herself from imagining orgasming with either, with both! She thought of marbles scattering across the room. She thought of confetti cannons and gymnastic ribbons. It was difficult for her to picture any balls.

Imagine threatening an artist and thinking they wouldn't respond. Imagine assuming they wouldn't have the time or energy. Sabine finished three glasses of wine, drinking them exactly how the spectre of creativity would. One, two, three: she banged the glass onto her desk each time, leaned back in her chair, and thrust her hips in the air.

Sabine took her time lighting another cigarette. After a few more intermittent thrusts, she set up her phone to live stream herself on TikTok and proceeded to outline the concept of the spectre of creativity to her followers. She very briefly explained the horror of being stalked, minimising only her emotional reaction to it.

"Look at my genius work," said Sabine, hiccupping.

She panned her phone across the wall of puppets. Past the skin of *Chubby Toddler* wearing a tutu, then the big-toothed earnestness of *Child*, then over the glittering face of *Preteen*. She panned down the length of *Depressive Young Adult*, which still emitted the strong scent of DKNY Be Delicious perfume from when it was last soaked.

Imbued with the spectre of creativity's energy, Sabine clicked her phone into the tripod and then unhooked the largest gothic skin from the wall. She held *Baby* under each of its armpits and lifted it towards the camera, trying to keep the head upright. The face was a circle of transparent silk laser-printed with a photo of Sabine as a newborn, mid-cry.

She demonstrated how to scrunch up the skin before sliding it on, as if putting on a pair of stockings. When she was fully encased, she repositioned the face of *Baby* so that it covered her own.

Y2KNostalgia commented: *Sis no take it off*

AstralProjection420 commented: *This is so Gemini coded*

TheGoetheGalleryOfficial commented: *Want to learn more about our artists and their fascinating work? Exhibition details for Fuck You, Help Me on our website. See you there!*

Gyal_with_the_Gyat commented: *Are these for sale?*

TheGoetheGalleryOfficial commented: *YES. Prints available after the exhibition, make sure you click the shop link on our website to discover Sabine's unnerving self-portraits.*

Gyal_with_the_Gyat commented: *She looks like Danny De-Vito as the Penguin*

Inside the puppet it was warm. Sabine allowed a few seconds to pass before she became the baby. Although the audience wouldn't witness this, it was paramount to her process that she physically "jerk" into the character of the puppet. She engaged in a short exercise of "emptying out," which involved heavy breathing while simultaneously believing that the body was emptied.

Sabine sucked on her puppet thumb. She imagined people being completely torn asunder by this image. There would be so many screenshots. Sabine demonstrated how trepidatious she was by removing her thumb and saying, "Mama?" then quickly returning her hand to her mouth. This was repeated one hundred times.

AstralProjection420 commented: *This feels illegal*

CokeSniff commented: *Just spat out my drink*

CokeSniff commented: *Incredible commitment to the bit*

While still inhabiting *Baby,* Sabine showed everyone her new knife skills. She rehearsed running and jumping at someone. She kicked the back of her chair and attempted a vault off the desk. Sabine caught sight of herself being rowdy in the reflection of the studio window. The sky outside was blue-black. *Since when?* The moonlight lit the soggy garden. *Since when?*

It only took a few seconds for Sabine to see that beyond her reflection was a dark shape standing outside her studio window. The vapour from the shadow's breath misted the glass. The Rembrandt Man who took a step towards the glass.

Sabine drowned in choices that kept swooping in. The man stared at the phone in her hand, and she followed his gaze. He watched her phone light up, emojis and comments streaming like strands of DNA down the screen as people commented on her puppet skin. He refocused back on her face, narrowed his eyes, and thumped on the window with his fist. He took his jacket off, wrapped it around his arm and then pulled his hand back, ready to punch. Sabine screamed. The man outside froze and poised as if listening. She lifted her phone to her mouth until her lips and nose filled the screen.

"He's here!"

The man pulled his arm back once more and punched the window. The glass shattered in a silver spray into the middle of the room.

Sabine ran into the hallway, struggling to take *Baby* off. Four hundred and twenty-three people watched as she shed the skin, dropped her phone, hoisted her padded backpack onto her shoulder, swiped up the phone again and pelted down the street, leaving the door open. A car horn sounded on the main street ahead and Sabine spun around and almost turned to dust.

"I'm being hunted!" she yelled into the phone.

AliBabaFashionSlutzz commented: *Omfg she's going to die*

SweetFluffy commented: *Please put the phone down or hold it still*

AliBabaFashionSlutzz commented: *Don't go without a fight bb*

Sabine screamed. She ran, knees to the sky, knees to the sky.

Habibilungfish commented: *She's giving face tonight*

HockneyBlue commented: *Oh she's eatin*

PackingTape commented: *Me when my SSENSE package arrives*

CoolAndFine commented: *Me getting my ten thousand steps in*

CokeSniff commented: *Me when the comms/law ball tickets go on sale*

"This is real," Sabine yelled. "Are you guys kidding me?"

She held her phone close to her face as more gifts and roses and hearts flowed. The purr of soft trills from her phone. Sabine sprinted barefoot down the road towards the lights of the main street. Every time her heel hit the bitumen, the impact travelled all the way to her eyeballs. She was flying.

"Please can someone record this," Sabine said.

She held her phone up to capture the man if he came up behind her, but the street was quiet. She slowed to a jog. Slowly the man emerged from the front door of the house. He looked straight ahead as he opened the front gate and then stood on the street facing her. In one hand he gripped *Baby*, its nappy slipping off as he dragged it on the ground beside him.

Sabine screamed so loudly that the mucus was stripped from her throat.

"I need the police," Sabine said. She took a few steps backwards until she was standing on the footpath of the main road. The Rembrandt Man remained still. She pointed her phone at him, hoping to capture his face.

"Give me my baby back," said Sabine.

Zero.Absoluto commented: *Gifts and love from Italy bella*

SweetFluffy commented: *This is so insensitive for people who have actually experienced assault*

PackingTape commented: *I need your face care routine*

WheatGerm commented: *She already said she uses La Roche-Posay. It's in her saved clips*

HockneyBlue commented: *Please tell me you're going to burning man this year*

"This is not art," Sabine panted. "He's stolen a priceless art-work from my studio. I need an ambulance, I'm dying."

Her followers responded with emojis of eyes and hearts. People letting her know she was welcome at their houses. *You can come here*, they kept typing.

"This is the man I was telling you about who's stalking me and—" Sabine stopped.

The man started to run in her direction. *Baby*'s nappy flew off, lost to the wind, the puppet's chubby legs now flapping like streamers behind him.

Sabine squealed.

Strong.Fit.Serbian44 commented: *Sexy angry girl*

Strong.Fit.Serbian44 commented: *The man not there relax*

Pignut666 commented: *She's so healing to watch like she's not self conscious about her stomach at all*

PackingTape commented: *I recognise this street*

KibbleJoy commented: *She lives in Brunswick*

Pignut666 commented: *No, she used to, but she moved*

Sabine ran down the main road. Standing at the intersec-tion, she held her phone out in front of her face, speaking into it. She scanned her eyes from house to house. The man had vanished. She sniffed the air. Nothing.

"Can you send me the footage, anything you've got," said Sabine.

WheatGerm commented: *She's so real for this*

KibbleJoy commented: *No one here gets performance art*

Feast_of_Wolves commented: *Goethe putting pressure on their artists to go viral for marketing. The art world is sick*

Sabine's inbox pinged with pieces of recorded footage. Each clip was blurry, and the only clear sounds were her ragged breathing and the rasp of her arms rubbing against her sides. She scrolled to the next clip, but it was the same. They were all the same.

TheGoetheGalleryOfficial commented: *What a thought-pro-voking piece Sabine provided for us this evening. Brings to mind such questions as what fear is, why we run, who the man represents, what is considered safe—and so many more! Great work tonight, Sabine. We were all right there with you. Brava! (Dare we say, encore?)*

The Last Thing I Said to You
Was Don't Leave Me Here II

—TRACEY EMIN, 2000

In the early hours of Saturday morning, Sabine walked towards the closest police station, keeping under the awning lights and close to the restaurants. Her phone battery was low. Ruth was not answering her phone. There was no word from Constantine, even though she had sent him multiple messages. He often went to late-night bars after his Friday-night shifts. These were places open only to hospitality staff, to decompress, like deepwater diving bells. All that sticky arancini and bloody pinot. Industry bars were for libertines and hedonists. They were for singletons. Sabine imagined him laughing (laughing!), ordering more drinks, and turning ruddy with booze and joy.

Sabine bought a portable phone charger from the petrol station. She plugged her phone into the battery and stood near the sliding doors, under the brightest lights. In small, sinister ways, she saw herself from every external angle. His gaze had become her own.

Sabine walked the rest of the distance to the police station. Lightning flickered nearby and rain pelted the brick building until sheets of water spilled from the gutters. Inside the foyer, a bucket that was already half-full caught a dribbling leak. Behind Sabine were the lead pencil–punctured, vinyl-covered seats for the public. The only other people there were an old Greek man holding a black eye, a shopping trolley beside him, and a teenager in cutoff shorts finger-drumming against her own thighs.

Sabine explained the night's happenings to the female officer who, unperturbed, took notes diligently.

"Where are the letters?" said the female officer, sighing.

"I can't find them," said Sabine.

Two male officers wandered over. They stood on either side of the female officer and asked Sabine to explain everything from the beginning. The male officer to the right cocked his head as he listened, while the other nodded in what Sabine thought looked like studied sympathy.

"You said he stole an artwork. Can you tell me the dimensions of the painting and describe it for me?" said the cocked-head officer.

"It was a sculpture of her baby," said the female officer.

"How big?" said the nodding officer.

"Seven feet," said Sabine.

"You have pictures?" said the cocked-head officer.

"There's not anything we can really do," said the nodding one, "unless you call us the next time he's there."

Their reluctance to work was palpable.

The three officers stood in a line like carollers and took turns telling Sabine different tactics to stay safe. She should take different routes to and from the house, look out for suspicious behaviour, and never wear headphones while walking. She shouldn't ever be in an unlocked house alone, and they warned against posting her location on social media. *Who do you live with? Who can you call to pick you up? Can you have a male family member stay? Can you get the phone numbers of any neighbours?*

"Don't confront him," the tallest officer said. "Don't engage at all. Stalkers love engagement."

"But then again, if he feels ignored he might escalate things, there's a phenomenon called extinction burst," said the female officer.

Sabine pressed the fingernails of her left hand into the palm of her right.

"Try not to touch any evidence. Pick the letters up by pinching one corner so we can submit them for forensic testing," said the officer taking notes.

"We could send a car around now, but I guarantee you he's long gone."

"Twenty minutes is our average callout time."

As Sabine signed a formal report, she disassociated from the experience. Like a yolk sucked from an eggshell by a weasel, her body cracked open and out she flowed. Was it a budgeting thing that they couldn't do more? Was it a law thing? No one explained.

Outside the police station, Sabine set the timer on her phone for twenty minutes. She imagined the Rembrandt Man breaking in and racing towards her and then grabbing each of her shoulders like tennis balls and knocking her body repeatedly against the wall until her head cracked. She pictured him swinging open the bathroom door as she stood in the shower; in shock, she slipped on the tiles, her legs bending outwards like those of a newborn foal. Sabine imagined she could be impossibly quicker or receive cosmic luck, but the elastic of reality snapped her back each time. The police would never get to her fast enough.

As the timer on her phone sounded, she understood why the young queen, Catherine Howard, had asked for the block to be brought to her chamber in the Tower of London the night before her execution. Each time Sabine thought of her attacker, she was laying her neck on the block, preparing, in one of the only ways she could, for the final, hideous thwack.

Orgy for Ten People in One Body

—ISABELLE ALBUQUERQUE, 2022

At the twenty-four-hour McDonald's, under those fluorescent lights that made raw meat of her skin, Sabine connected to the Wi-Fi and plugged in her headphones. It was three thirty in the morning. This beacon of capitalism became a welcome home. It smelled of dishwashing steam and hot fat, and had as much salt in the air as a coastal town. Greasy fingerprints and sugar granules covered her table. Under the constant eyes of the security cameras, Sabine could relax.

She propped her elbows on the table and rested her head in her hands, barely noticing the possum-pink-eyed customers, drunk, tired, or high from their Saturday evenings, line up, swaying as they took turns to order. She was too busy positioning herself on the conveyor belt of the internet. Sabine opened her eyes and let the content roll in. She began with tactical masks. Masks made of wool. Eye holes? Balaclavas. Ski masks! Duct tape. Safety plans. The first page of the psychology of

stalking handbook. The minutiae of a stalking victim's final
walk. The letters from Whitney Houston's FBI file. Victim impact statements. A comprehensive guide to writing your own
victim impact statement. What you should remove from your
victim impact statement. *Ten Terrifying Cases of Sadistic Stalkers.* More names. More cases. MORE NAMES. MORE CASES.

Sabine refreshed the long list of thumbnails that reloaded
under the heading, *Intruder Porn. Sexy girl in white socks
fucked by intruder. INTRUDER entered my room and I ended up
liking his cock! Two lesbian robbers fuck. College Student Fucks
for Her Life When Robber Breaks In.* Sabine fast-forwarded
through each of them, watching in triple speed. When one
intruder positioned a woman into a crawling position, Sabine
paused the clip and hovered her finger above the image of the
woman looking directly into the camera and took a screenshot. *Chun-cluck, chun-cluck, chun-cluck.* The shutter cut the
images from the internet and dropped them into the roaring
fire that burned so high inside her that it singed the bottom of
her brain.

Our Heads Are Round So Our Thoughts Can Change Direction

—FRANCIS PICABIA, 1922

At sunrise, Sabine ordered a cab home. She expected Constantine to be home, but instead she entered a freezing, empty house. Wind whistled through the shattered window of her studio. She pulled the curtain and placed a chair in front of it, pinning the fabric to the wall. Large triangular pieces of broken glass spread across the room. The glittering shards trailed from the floor beneath the window all the way to her desk. Sabine knelt down and picked up the largest pieces first. She piled them into her hand and then wrapped them in paper and put them into the waste bin. She fetched the dustpan and brush from the laundry and swept up the rest. Finally, as she ran the vacuum over the floor, she saw she was bleeding. Her knees ran rivulets of blood from kneeling on the floor and the palms of her hands were sliced with thin cuts.

On her way to the laundry to fetch Band-Aids, Constantine arrived home. He braced himself against the wall as he kicked off one shoe and then the other, which landed several feet away. A half-finished bottle of Gatorade bulged in his pant pocket.

"My phone died," he said.

Sabine stood, silent. He said nothing about how frigidly cold the house was.

"My love, you're bleeding," he said.

Sabine poured out everything that had happened. She told him about her majestic cock and the spectre of creativity and pounding her exhibition and then wearing *Baby*. She took a breath. She told him about how at first she was just being fully present with her followers and then the man had smashed the glass with his fist and come in, and she'd had to run.

Constantine listened, his eyes widening with each detail. He left her briefly to look into her study but quickly came back.

She smiled in a relaxed way at her husband, hoping the smile was reassuringly sane. She wanted him to believe that truth flowed naturally from her. She wiped her hands on her shirt and then slid them into her back pockets. The cuts hurt against the fabric of her pants.

"All this blood is yours?" said Constantine. He stooped over to inspect a large patch where it had begun to brown. He touched his fingers to it. He tried to wipe it with his bare hand.

"I've just spread it around by walking through it," said Sabine.

"Show me your hands," he said. He stood in front of her and waited until she removed her hands from her pockets and then he gently inspected them. The friction had caused the cuts to bleed again. Her body was betraying her.

"What have you done to yourself?" he said. He tilted her palms into the light.

"I told you, I was in there cleaning up the broken window," said Sabine.

Constantine wasn't listening. He lifted both of her hands to his face. She could see his lips were stained from red wine. He smelled faintly of onions.

"Most of the bleeding has stopped," said Sabine.

"This is no good," he said. He looked at her, his forehead wrinkled with concern.

"I didn't do this to myself. It was the glass," said Sabine. Naming it made her seem unafraid of how it looked. Preempt and reassure.

"I couldn't find gloves," said Sabine.

Constantine opened his mouth to say something but she interrupted him.

"Or a broom."

He turned her hands over to look at the back of them, then held them palms up. Sabine watched Constantine compose his thoughts. Everything about him was shadowed by doubt.

"Glass will be glass," she said, and as soon as it was out of her mouth she knew that he might suspect she was not all right. *Glass will be glass?* What she should have said was something like: *A little blood never hurt anybody.*

"Let's sit," said Constantine.

"A little blood never," began Sabine, but she had to stop as she was already crying.

He placed his arm across her shoulders and steered her towards the dining table. He pulled out a chair and lowered her into it, and left her there momentarily before returning with a blanket and some socks. He wrapped the blanket around her, then unballed the socks, crouched down, and pulled them onto her freezing feet. The socks were tight and dug into her ankles.

Sabine sat at the table, her hands throbbing, as Constantine bustled about. He brought her a cup of tea. He placed two pieces of toast into the toaster and then pulled up a seat next to her. Sabine stared at his clean chequered pants. She could smell his deodorant had just been freshly applied. He had brushed his teeth.

"Are you going to work again?" said Sabine.

"I need to," said Constantine.

"You didn't even come home," said Sabine.

"I told you it was Sven's leaving drinks. The man has a drinking problem. Oh no, no, no, why are you crying?" said Constantine.

"I'm not," said Sabine, bawling.

Constantine stood and popped the toast prematurely, then buttered it on the bench without a plate. He placed both slices, one stacked on top of the other, in front of her. Melted butter dripped from the bread to the table. Constantine told her he would organise for his cousin to fix the glass. He said, "Don't worry, my love, don't worry." He said, and this surprised Sabine, "These things happen."

"Do they?" said Sabine.

Within the hour, the cousin came with his glazier's van and the house was sealed shut. Sabine thought the new glass seemed thinner, weaker. Constantine didn't agree but when she tapped on it, and when she tried to scratch it with her fingernail, it felt like plastic.

Constantine left, claiming he would return earlier than usual. He kissed her head and her cheek, and turned back twice to look at Sabine as he walked down the hall towards the front door.

"I'm loving you, very, very hard, can you feel it?" he called out to her.

"No," said Sabine, more to herself than him. She took a bite of cold toast and closed all the curtains.

When Ruth responded to her call with hysteria, Sabine was relieved. She arrived at the house with Lou, a long-handled axe, and an evil eye. She sat on the sofa next to Lou, her axe resting across her feet, watching while Sabine reclined in the armchair, holding the eye on her lap. She insisted that Sabine tell her everything from the start. As she listened, she held Lou's hand, groaned, and drew shaky breaths. This was the expected response. This was appropriate.

"Are you really okay?" said Ruth.

"Not at all," said Sabine.

Lou inspected the doors and windows.

"You're actually fucked," he said.

Sabine tucked the evil eye into her desk drawer, then showed Lou her knives. She revealed weapons behind cushions and pot plants. A thumping piece of driftwood. Seven large river rocks. More clanging, glinting knives.

"We need to talk about the knives," said Lou. "It's completely illegal to introduce a weapon into an altercation. You need to ditch them."

"But keep the rocks," said Ruth.

"Surely if he breaks into my house, legally I have right of way with the knives?" said Sabine.

"If it went to court you would look really bad. It would seem premeditated. You might be able to give a reason for the meat cleaver to be in your studio, and the driftwood would probably be okay, but I'm counting—what is it, eight knives? It's suspicious."

"Where's that heavy vase?" said Ruth.

Lou removed a silver pen from his pocket and clicked off the lid. "If I used this, it would be self-defence, because this is nothing, it's a small pen, but if I am in a threatening situation where my life is on the line then I can use this like a knife."

"Get out your pens!" said Ruth.

"You wouldn't be able to cut cheddar with that," said Sabine.

"You've got a boning knife hanging by a piece of wool from the back of your chair," said Lou.

"Why did you bring me an axe, then?" said Sabine.

"It's for chopping wood. You put it next to the stack of wood on the fireplace and hope he attacks you there," said Ruth.

"You know we don't have a fireplace," said Sabine.

"People light fires, though, that's a normal thing. People toast marshmallows and drink their warm milk beside small fires they make at home. You can buy firepits from the hardware store," said Ruth.

"Put a plate in your studio with a half-cut apple on it and put the paring knife next to that," said Lou.

"Just an innocent snack," said Ruth.

"Make it look real—precut some pieces, and change the apple daily so it's not old," said Lou.

"A little snack," said Sabine.

"A really sharp, permanent snack," said Lou.

"And remember you're cold, so you're always chopping wood, for the sharp little fire that you're one day preparing to light," said Ruth.

Shadow of Men

—CLEON PETERSON, 2018

By lunchtime, Ruth and Lou had left, but between seeing them out the door and finding a spot for the axe, she had received another letter:

> *You are a very dangerous, sneaky person. You were mocking me dressed in that costume like a freak. You baited me but I am a shark not a fucking fish. Women like you are garbage. You stink you reek you repulse me. I want to—should I even say? What I want to do is shove you into that big baby costume and tie the ends closed. Every time you try to get out I'll put you back in. Now that is not a bad idea for an artwork. Imagine—I'm laughing now—but imagine a celebrated ignorant whore of an artist dying like that it's pure art do you agree?*

Sabine sat at the kitchen table and tore the letter into strips. Methodically she pinched the corner of the paper, like the cop had told her, between her thumb and forefinger, she then dragged one line at a time from the page, shredding his words into lines of nonsense. At first she made herself think about everything that spiked her anger. All the past lovers who had touched her, either politely or impolitely, without first checking to see if she wanted it. Everyone who had set a flag into the soft sand of her body and claimed it as their own. Galleries included. Art included. To the growing pile, Sabine added the memory of the convoy of young men in loud cars who tried to run her off the road one night. *For what purpose? What did all those men want with her in a ditch?* The gallerist who had told her there was a hollowness inside the skull of every young artist. *Maybe right?* The art collector who only bought work from young brunette female emerging artists, and with every transaction demanded a hug. *But was that weird?* The night she saw a group of men in an alley punching a crying woman. *How did she know she was crying if it was dark?* Another night, when she saw an entirely different group of men chasing a smaller man. The time she was followed from the train station in the middle of the day. *He could have been going the same direction.* The man who ran after her and insisted she give her number to him. *Didn't he look like Danny Trejo and didn't she want to, though?* The bartender who made her cocktail extra strong and then again and again. The friend who said she was good at a lot of things but great at none. *Perhaps right?* Shitty paintings of faces and fruit that sold for ten times more than her own work. Curators and galleries, the public! Anyone who had told her no thank you, not this time. Tight dresses and public changerooms. Artist statements. Screw those statements. Screw this life. She looked around the room. Screw that uncomfortable chair and the blunt blender and the spoon too wide for her mouth and that pathetic excuse for Greek yogurt and literally every muscle in her body that was hurting and not working for the greater good of her body. Shredding the letter was a warning to all inanimate things. A little reminder that it could all be dismantled. She was threatening everything.

Sabine tore the letter until little tendrils covered the floor by her chair.

Truth Coming Out of Her Well

—JEAN-LÉON GÉRÔME, 1896

"Yoo-hoo!" The ghost of Carolee Schneemann stood outside the kitchen window, knocking on the glass with a lemon. She balanced a washing basket of lemons on her hip.

Sabine stood up and walked over to open the window, trailing pieces of the letter.

"Why are you nude?" said Sabine.

"I've got the roaches, and I've got my ribbons on," said Carolee. She gestured to her wrists and ankles where lengths of white silk were tied into bows.

"Constantine likes to leave some of the lemons in situ," said Sabine.

"It's going to get astonishingly weird for you between now and your exhibition," said Carolee.

"Weird is a really tricky word for me to unpack at the moment. Can you elaborate?" said Sabine.

"It's going to get spooky," said Carolee.

"Tell me what will happen," said Sabine.

"Lemons absolutely adore being picked, don't they?" said Carolee.

"Yeah, they love it," said Sabine.

"I'm coming in," said Carolee, handing Sabine the basket of lemons before squeezing through the open window and heading for the laundry.

"I can get you a sarong," said Sabine.

"Lemons were made to be sliced into our drinks, and juiced into curd, and squeezed over our fishes, do you agree?" said Carolee.

"Sure," said Sabine.

Sabine followed Carolee into the laundry and watched as she dumped the basket into the sink. Carolee blasted the tap. Sabine stood to her side, taking each lemon one at a time and twisting the fruit from its short, star-shaped stem before tossing it back into the sink to be with its siblings. When the lemons were clean, Carolee set out a cutting board on the dining table with two peelers.

"Can I ask you a question?" said Sabine.

"I would rather you didn't," said Carolee.

"What's bigger than a human being?" said Sabine.

"Only their own emotions about things, I would say," said Carolee.

"I mean gods, or aliens," said Sabine.

"Har har," said Carolee, snorting. "Hahahahaha!"

At the dining table, Sabine cleared space for them to sit by using her forearm to swipe the pomegranates to the floor. They sat opposite each other and peeled the rinds into a glass bowl. Sabine held on to the pithy flesh of her lemon so hard that it popped out of her hand and onto the floor, where she let it roll away. She dragged the peeler over the skin of another lemon, letting the citrus oils disperse.

Once the lemons were peeled, Carolee poured three cups of sugar into a pot of boiling water. She stirred it with an old wooden spoon until there were no granules in the liquid.

"Art is a living spell," said Carolee.

"It would make more sense if that were true," said Sabine.

"Give me his letters," said Carolee.

Sabine gathered the strips from the floor, wiping them clean of dust before handing them over.

"Before you ask, we are making limoncello," said Carolee. She poured the sugar syrup into a tall pot and then added all the rind. "Because you clearly like to drink too much." Carolee rattled the recycling bin, clinking the bottles and cans together.

Sabine dropped the pieces of the letter into the pot, where they floated on the surface until Carolee emptied in a bottle of vodka, sliding the pieces into liquid nothingness. With the wooden spoon, Sabine stirred the mixture until the paper disintegrated and there were only specks of white in the cloudy limoncello. The lengths of bright yellow skin rolled languidly like rope off a dock.

"You're less talkative today," said Sabine.

"I did not come all this way to simply talk to you." Carolee cupped a hand to her ear. "He's coming, can't you hear it?"

"Now?" said Sabine.

"May as well be," said Carolee.

Sabine fetched the empty glass bottles Constantine used for passata from the pantry. Carolee gripped the pot handles with the tea towel and poured the liquid into the bottles through a plastic funnel.

"I think it is now time for you to go outside," said Carolee.

"It's too cold," said Sabine.

Carolee walked to the laundry and removed a towel from the dirty hamper. She passed it to Sabine who wrapped it around herself then followed Carolee through the back door.

The Rembrandt Man had destroyed their garden. Every plant overturned in a tantrum. Flowers were shredded and scattered. Clumps of grass pulled like toupees from the dirt. Panic rose in Sabine. Boot imprints, deep and clear, tracked through the mud, and in the centre of it all was her gothic puppet *Baby*, left stuffed full of plants and dirt, and laid belly up, bloated, under the lemon tree.

Sabine picked her way through the carnage. She felt a rolling, internal tremor. If she opened her mouth, there would be a sucking sound at the top of her throat, behind her tonsils. Her anger filled her up and stretched her out. She tasted game and salt. She threw a net of nasturtiums out of her path and muddied her slippers by kicking away the flowering kale as she made her way to *Baby*.

Sabine wiped the dirt off the silk face. Her baby puppet's head gaped with holes. She reached in through its mouth to claw out crushed roses and lettuces, handfuls of snapped vines. Sabine cradled her baby, hugging the cold puppet against her chest.

"Bring me a blanket," said Sabine.

Carolee scooped *Baby* into a striped beach towel.

Sabine felt her bones and bowel and spleen, even her nervous system, swell and thicken. She lifted a hand to her neck; her neck was square, she was spreading.

"I'm going to tell you something, but you're not going to like it," said Carolee.

"Go ahead," said Sabine. She cradled *Baby*.

"There is a point where your fury can get so big that it becomes its own entity. It will grow a head and a torso and arms and legs depending on how angry you are, but the bigger it gets the harder it is to control. It's a beast then, and it never wants to be small again."

"My fury is already as big as that," said Sabine.

"It's getting there. You need to be very careful. Once the entity is big enough, it cannot be dismantled. It's stronger than you. It stands inside you and wears you like a cloak. Sabine, it will wear your hands as gloves."

"A demon?" said Sabine.

"It's strong enough to pull out your leg bones and push its own in. It moves you around, makes you look in the mirror and see only it, an inch under your skin. When you lock eyes in the mirror, its eyes look back. 'Look how big I grew,' the eyes will say. And if the eyes don't, the mouth will. You will wake in the night to hear it snoring through your own lips, its tongue animated even when it sleeps, flopping, poking, rolling in your own wet mouth."

"I feel it," said Sabine.

"It wheezes. Coughs. Gasps. It's so full inside you, there is not enough space for you both to sleep, both to breathe. And when it wakes, it heaves you out of bed. It will walk you down this corridor to this bathroom and turn the light on, only to stare at itself again in the mirror. It will love how big it grew."

"Is that what happened to you?" said Sabine.

"You need to keep it as small as possible," said Carolee.

Sabine's stomach burbled. She stood and burped. She bent over and retched. Inside, her fear and fury ripened, then began to rot.

Tribute to Ana Mendieta

—TANIA BRUGUERA, 1985–96

Sabine searched her body for normalcy and eradicated it. She used Constantine's beard comb to tease her hair into a tangled beehive on top of her head. She pulled strands of hair out from the nest and curled them into bouncing ringlets. She added ribbons and clips and more combs, and then sprayed it until it was hydrophobic from hairspray.

Sabine dipped a makeup brush into a pot of face powder and dusted her pallid face until it was white. She filed her nails into points, then dipped the tips of her fingernails into a bottle of blue ink. She stuck out her tongue and dripped the ink into her mouth, staining her teeth. She poured silver paint into teacups and then dipped her elbows. She admired herself in the full-length mirror. She was art. It had happened in only fifteen minutes. She banged doors open and shut with the force that pulsed through her body of work. She dropped things out of her objet d'art hands. She fed her hungry objet d'art belly with granulated coffee by the spoonful and green jelly crystals, which she washed down with black tea and the last of the liquid iron tonic.

Before she knew how to make puppets, Sabine had made other things. Often, she didn't know what she was making until many hours into the piece, when she would finally step back and look at the work, and realise it was a human figure, or a strange chair, or a precious pile of similar objects. There was one particular sculpture that didn't reveal itself to her for weeks. She worked on it every night, head down, hands busy, and when she finally stepped back she saw she had made a boat to sink herself in. She threw it into the communal bins, scared that she might become so bewitched by the work that one night she would wake up and find herself cresting waves in her sculpture.

Sabine placed the blue tip of her finger in the middle of a trail of ants running from a damp crack in the plaster to an orange patch of stickiness near the kettle. Finding their line blocked, the ants whirled in chaos, but soon fell into a new line, flowing around her finger. Sabine slid her finger to the side to block them a second time. Distressed, they scurried to re-form a steady line around her again. Sabine removed her finger.

The story the Rembrandt Man was telling himself was that he was pursuing her, which made her frightened of him. He was writing a role for her that was becoming more and more horrific. If he attacked her, then she was attacked. Sabine slid her finger into the line of ants once more.

The man's essence still clogged her garden. Her new hands pointed it out to her. His spirit lingered, haunting her. Sabine fetched her phone, shed her clothes, then swung the back door open and stalked into the garden. She faced her tripod towards the patch of dirt that she and Constantine were preparing for winter planting, attached her phone to the lock, and live streamed herself as she walked in front of the lens.

Under the bruised, rain-heavy clouds, Sabine shoved branches and incredulity out of her way. She stomped over a section of the pumpkin vine, flattening its hollow stem with a thick crunch. She slapped a flowering artichoke out of her path until she stood right in the middle of tufts of rhubarb. Elephant grass and flowers flanked her, and an unholy number of snails. Behind her a bush of rank-smelling daisies shook in the wind. The sky leaked in a steady drizzle. She squirmed. Her fury uncoiled, straightened, and lengthened. It took over any spare space inside. It sizzled and crackled.

Sabine walked in a large figure of eight that encompassed the whole garden, caressing the remaining plants. She cooed to insects, which bobbed out of her way. As a breeze picked up, Sabine raised her arms above her head and twinkled her fingers, letting the fresh wind touch all areas of her skin. She moved in a wide circle until she was standing in front of the phone again.

Sabine's skin constricted in the cold. Her atoms remembered something she couldn't. She had given away her hands. At the base of the lemon tree, Sabine bent at the waist then dug into the mineral earth, using her nails to claw and shovel the rich brown soil into a mound behind her. Her breathing turned to a rasp. Sabine dribbled as she scrabbled and scraped, digging the hole until it was as deep as her forearms. She placed a foot either side of the hole, hugged her thighs to her chest in a squat, screamed at the sky, and shat.

Ginormous bats tumbled out of the overhead branches

to see her offering. Sabine was now part of the garden's ecosystem. She had successfully elbowed her way into the cycle of flora and fauna. This was an exchange between her and terra firma. She too was made from rocks and bark, mulch and nasturtiums, and whatever else was lying around. Cosmic comets and waving fields of wheat, bushfires and gushing cinnamon-coloured floodwaters. Star dust. Mica. Sap and pollen. She wasn't a human body, she was elemental. Sabine was flipping and gliding, morphing and beaming through the particles of everything surrounding her. The sharp slap of creativity smarted.

The shit was authentic, it was animalistic. This was a territorial shit. It zinged with transcendence. Everything else she had ever made was embarrassing compared with this. This genuine art. This materia prima. It was divine. Her shit was holy.

Sabine stood. She was a galleon in full sail. She walked towards the camera and turned her live stream off. Patti Smith said the night belonged to lovers, but that wasn't true—the night was hers.

The Guest

—JULIE CURTISS, 2018

Every Saturday night, Constantine's restaurant, Small Mother, served the fattest rock oysters in the city. They were arranged on a platter of shaved ice with a dressing made from Crimson Tide finger limes, smoked salt, and yuzu. People flocked to the restaurant to publicly open their mouths like gropers and flick them down their necks.

Small Mother was an opulent shrine to modernism. It was designed around the open kitchen, which was raised on a platform like a theatre stage. The banging and sizzling drowned out the birds, who sat outside screeching at the onset of dusk. The seating area, full of people, was a subterranean chamber of metal, wood, and stone. It featured oak furniture, indoor shrubbery, a concrete ceiling, and low lighting. Through the windows, Sabine watched the rain continue to pelt the already sodden grass.

The energy drinks and caffeine pills had left her buzzing

and high but too ravenous to think. She was shown to her table by a waiter wearing a leather apron. She took her seat then smoothed her hand across the heavy tablecloth and placed her napkin across her lap. The cleanness of the cloth highlighted how dirty she was. Her linen pants were covered in ink stains and coffee spills. Her fingertips were vivid blue, and there was a crescent of soil under each of her fingernails. Sabine ran her tongue over her teeth, wondering if they were still coated in the film of blue ink.

A waiter took her order, and Sabine listed the first things she saw on the menu. The crab. The quail. The radicchio salad. Wood-fired focaccia with truffle butter. A beer. A cosmopolitan. The waiter diligently wrote it down, and then returned, placing her beer on a napkin and the plate of bread in the centre of the table.

"Can you let the chef know I'm here?" Sabine lifted the glass and drank until beer ran out the sides of her mouth and down her chin. She wiped her face on her sleeve, then sighed and burped.

"Excuse me, I'm so thirsty," she said.

"Who shall I say is here?" the waiter asked. He took her empty glass.

"His calm and loving wife," she said. *Was it hot?* She was feverish.

Sabine tore a piece of bread and buttered it, specks of truffle like dirt through the yellow. It tasted earthy, like licking moss from the forest floor. She shoved more in. With her mouth full, Sabine noticed Constantine looking over at her from the kitchen. He held up a finger, as if to say, *One minute.*

When he finally arrived, he placed her cosmopolitan in

front of her and threw a tea towel over his shoulder. To her relief, he sat down opposite her.

"Are you pleased to see me?" she said. She lifted the cosmo to her mouth and drank until it was gone.

"I am glad you came," he said. He retightened the strap of his watch.

She placed her hand on top of the table in case he wanted to hold it.

"I'm not sure I've ever seen your hair like this," Constantine said.

Sabine patted down her scratchy hair. Her mind was glue. There was nothing in her glass. Nothing for her to talk about. Dead space between them. She wanted to ask Constantine what was happening to them, but questions like this confused him.

"Nails look good," he said. Sabine tucked her fingers away. Her nails were cupboards on the end of her fingers to keep parts of the Rembrandt Man in. Sabine couldn't even remember the last time she had slept.

"Do you want to talk about anything?" she said.

"Not really. It's getting busier, I'd better go," he said.

Constantine's reluctance to understand that she was being stalked embedded itself like a tick under her skin. Sabine fought the urge to tell him that their marriage had become a bowl of loose ends—sticky tape that kept tearing at the wrong point, keys to no identifiable door, loose nuts and loose change.

"I came here because the house is unsafe for me to be in. I have created an installation in the yard that will function as a spell. And while I'm here, I'm going to be fully transparent with you, so you know where I am coming from: I have been talking about my approach to art and fury with the ghost of

Carolee Schneemann," said Sabine. She waited for his intrigue and understanding.

"I swear the week you exhibit is like watching someone go through a prolonged psychosis," said Constantine.

"A what?" Sabine said, before squealing and liquifying in front of him, bubbling to the floor in offence.

"I'm concerned about your inability to deal with pressure, you are dis-regulated for months," said Constantine. He pulled the towel from his shoulder to his lap. He wasn't wearing his ring. He pushed his chair back and stood.

"Where's your wedding ring?" she said.

He stopped and looked at his hand.

"I take it off at work," he said, frowning at her.

"I'm going to confront the Rembrandt Man," she said. She hated the way his chair was pulled out and empty like that. Wouldn't he stay longer?

"Who?" said Constantine.

"My stalker," said Sabine.

Constantine sighed heavily. "You know what I always say? You cannot wrestle with a pig, because you will both end up covered in mud and the pig will love it. If this man exists, he will love it."

"*If*?" Sabine's jaw dropped. "I think I'm going to pass out." She held on to the edge of her chair with both hands.

"Sabine, this is my workplace." He spoke clearly but she barely heard him. Constantine stepped towards her, opening his arms for a hug, but she no longer wanted a hug from him.

Sabine kicked the table leg.

"Listen to me," he said, pointing his finger at her like a child. "We are not making a scene here."

"He's going to come in. And what then?" she said. "Use your

imagination. What do you think this man, *who exists*, is going to do to me?"

He clasped a hand onto her shoulder and held it there tightly. "Stop ruining everything," he said, squeezing her.

"Did you even know," she said, twisting away from him, her fists like cannonballs, "that I took a course to learn how to get away from someone trying to rape me? Did you know this?"

"I swear to God," said Constantine. He let go of her shoulder.

"Unhand me," she said.

"I'm not even touching you," he said. Constantine stepped back and raised both arms in surrender. "Take a breath," he said, his eyes wide and wary. "Keep it together, girl."

"Don't even worry, boy," she said.

Sabine held her napkin to her mouth and screamed until her head shook from the effort.

Small Beasts

—LOUISE HOWARD, 2022

Sabine arrived back at the house, sobbing, cramming a souvlaki into her mouth in a bid to overpower his truffles with something else. Her throat clogged with flatbread and chewy lamb. She let herself into the house, raced down the hall, and heaved into the bathroom sink, startling the ghost of Carolee Schneemann, who was sitting in the bath. Sabine perched on the toilet lid, wiping her mouth, and watched Carolee roll around in the water. She asked Sabine to add some scented oils to the water. Sabine shook a bottle of lavender oil onto Carolee's crepe-skinned legs until Carolee asked her several times to stop.

"A body is a powerful thing." Carolee kicked a leg out of the tub, splashing water across the tiles.

"You're not behaving like a ghost," said Sabine, "and it bothers me."

"Your mind is so rigid," said Carolee. She sank beneath the

water and let her breath billow out of her mouth and burst across the surface.

"No one is behaving as they should," said Sabine.

"You are," said Carolee.

"You shouldn't even technically be breathing," said Sabine.

"Stop oppressing me. I do what I want. I did not slog through my entire life making art only to die and be told I can't haunt the way I haunt," said Carolee.

"Constantine is going to leave me," said Sabine.

"You made such a tremendous scene, and it wasn't even art," said Carolee.

"He thinks I'm making up the Rembrandt Man," said Sabine.

"Yikes, what a dummy," said Carolee.

She drew her knees to her chest as the bathwater around her lit up. It was as if someone had dropped in a string of fairy lights. Sabine leaned over the edge of the bath to look. Surrounding Carolee were ugly brown fish with huge, down-turned mouths full of sharp teeth. A long fin with a light extended from each of their snouts. They drifted through the water, bumping into the walls of the tub, and each other.

"Piranhas?" Sabine asked.

"Anglerfish," said Carolee. She stroked the back of one as it swam past her.

"Absolute monsters," said Sabine.

"You know, in the darkest part of the sea, the female anglerfish attracts a mate by using her bioluminescence, which streams out from her head via this here lamp made from bacteria." Carolee grabbed a fish by the belly and held it up for Sabine to look at its head apparatus.

"This is a fake fish," said Sabine.

Carolee dumped it back into the water with a splash.

"And the males travel alone. They essentially spend their whole life trying to find the radiant light of a partner fish. We can imagine a fellow's relief when he finally finds her, can't we?"

"Show me the fish again," said Sabine.

Carolee tried to grab the closest one, but it swam away. She tried once more, but the fish were spooked and they pooled at her ankles. She gave up.

"And the female is significantly larger than the male. If they were human, the female would be able to carry the male on her hip. If she is seven inches, he is one inch. Through size alone, his female is majestic. Briny Gaia in all her luminescent glory."

"I love that the women fish are huge," said Sabine.

"The male finds his life partner and is overcome, and in his excitement he bites into her body and doesn't let go. His tiny jaw fuses to her wide abdomen and for some reason she allows it," said Carolee.

"She needs to shake him off," said Sabine.

"Hush. Now, over time the male anglerfish lets his organs atrophy. His eyes get reabsorbed, because she will see for him. He becomes too weak to swim, and his fins flounder, then fall still."

"Avoidable from the start," said Sabine.

"Their blood vessels join, making one circulatory system. The male no longer recognises hunger, because his female feeds him from her body. In return, she absorbs all the parts of him that are no longer necessary."

Carolee pulled the plug and let the water and the fish drain out. She stood up and gestured for Sabine to hand her a towel. Goose bumps rippled across her body, flocking from her thighs to her stomach.

"Bye-bye!" she said to the last fish, which circled the drain rapidly before slipping through the stopper in a whoosh.

"Contrary to what your eyes would tell you, the male is not dead, but he is forever stuck," she said. "How do you separate from your own blood? If he broke away from her, they would both die. She would be left with a wound too big to heal, and they would both sink to the ocean floor. Do you see what I am saying here?"

"Who is the male fish in this scenario?" said Sabine.

"It's clearly Constantine," said Carolee.

"That was not clear to me. I assumed you were talking about the Rembrandt Man, and I was sitting here thinking that if I were that big-mama fish I would wait until he was weak but not enough to hurt me, then I would shake him off and swim away," said Sabine.

"We are talking about your husband," said Carolee.

"I'm too intuitive to let us both—" said Sabine.

"Hurt each other in the most catastrophic way possible?" said Carolee.

Dogs Which Cannot Touch
Each Other

—PENG YU AND SUN YUAN, 2003

Sabine woke the next morning from sleeping sideways across the double bed. Constantine's pants were next to the clothes hamper. She pulled on a jumper then padded to the living room. On the couch, the spare blanket and Constantine's pillow were bundled up into a pile. She checked the time. It was still before nine. He had left early for work and not said goodbye. She sat on his pillow and tried to ring him. Voicemail. She tried seven more times with no luck. She lowered her phone from her ear as an incoming message tone sounded.

Cecily: *Good morning! How are you faring? Your messages last night about fury and fish were hilarious. Viva La Fuck You, Help Me! Show TOMORROW. See you at least an hour before opening.*

Cecily again: *Freya just told me you went live taking a shit in the yard—is this correct?*

Sabine didn't reply. She put her face into her husband's

pillow and inhaled. Woodsmoke. Scalp oil. Camphor. Tangy and sweet. He had always, to her at least, smelled like the most beautiful thing in the world. The man was a campsite at dusk. She lay face down on his pillow and breathed in again.

Two-Headed

—TSCHABALALA SELF, 2023

By 11:00 a.m. Sabine had done almost nothing except over-pluck her eyebrows. She stood at the kitchen sink and watched the garden through the window. The plants were menacing. Every bushel of leaves became an angry moving face. Bark hung as if torn from each trunk in dense tufts. It waved, beckoning her out. The droopy florets of the echinaceas looked impaled onto their stalks. Heads on sticks. Lorikeets screeched. Sabine lifted her wineglass to her lips, drained the glass, then poured herself another.

The sound of laughter floated down the hall and, as if it had legs, entered the kitchen. Sabine stopped chugging wine. The laughter stopped. A magpie warbled its morning song, and a neighbour began mowing their lawn.

She pulled a slice of bread from the bag and ate it. Sundays were usually her supermarket shopping days, but today she was too busy mentally preparing for her exhibition. She was required, for promotional purposes, to mobilise and turn herself inside out. She stood, chewing. She clawed through the bag for another slice. The sound of laughter started again. She lowered the bread from her mouth. It stopped. She raised her hand and took a bite.

She sent a message to Constantine, apologising for the scene at Small Mother. Shortly afterwards, she sent another message, telling him he would regret all the time they spent fighting. Then she sent another telling him she did truly love him. Another saying his reluctance to meet her in her vulnerability was because of his upbringing: it was his family's fault that he couldn't handle her emotionality. She forwarded him an essay on intimacy. She called his phone and hung up a dozen times. Rang his work. Rang his sister, whom she never rang. When Constantine didn't pick up or reply to her messages, she sent a message saying that she wished he would screw her like she wanted—hard, and with her face to the wall. She sent one final message telling him that she was worried she might be depressed.

Sabine sent Ruth a voice note of her singing "With a Little Help from My Friends." Ruth texted to say she had accidentally deleted it before she could listen all the way through. Sabine continued to be colonial in her attempts to disrupt. She harangued Lou for memes—*dank* memes, specifically. Lou asked if she wanted the "dankest of the dank," which Sabine found flirtatious. She sent back a message telling him to give her the essence of his generation or die, which he immediately hearted, but forgot to otherwise respond to.

Constantine rang.

"What is going on?" he said.

"You or I need to apologise for last night," said Sabine.

"When did you last sleep?" said Constantine.

Sabine couldn't remember.

"Where are your bath pearls? Your aromatherapy eye pillow?" said Constantine.

"It's not safe to have a bath unless you're home with me," said Sabine.

"Keep me on the phone and run a bath," said Constantine.

Sabine was silent.

"Come on. I want to hear that tap running," said Constantine.

"A bath is only going to waste my time," said Sabine.

"You're slurring. You're that tired you're slurring," said Constantine.

"I don't need sleep, I need to be ticking things off my list," said Sabine.

"What list?" said Constantine.

Sabine couldn't really say because there was no physical list, rather it was the idea of completing a series of things that would support the smooth running of her exhibition. She remained silent.

"Get the pearls," said Constantine.

Sabine walked to the bathroom and blasted the hot tap. She watched it spiral down the drain.

"Oh beautiful, I can hear you're doing it. You'll feel so much better afterwards," said Constantine.

"You're right, I will," said Sabine.

"FaceTime me so I can keep watch and so you feel safe," said Constantine.

"I'm just adding the pearls now," said Sabine. She stood motionless in the steam.

"Wonderful, my love. Throw in a handful for me," said Constantine.

"I'm going to get in now," said Sabine.

"I'm proud of you for taking care of yourself like this," said Constantine.

Sabine hung up the phone.

Sabine shut the tap off and wandered back to the living room. As she reclined across the sofa she created a social media account with the username RigorousArtist. For her bio she wrote: *Art is life.* Her profile picture was of one eyeball. Sabine uploaded pictures of her face and body. Photos of her hands holding things, like the edge of a rug or a glass ashtray. This was her new aesthetic. It was juicy and young. She was fresh as a mango. She friended Nick Cave and his wife, Susie, Emily Ratajkowski, as well as Constantine, Ruth, and the Goethe Gallery. She friended herself and liked all her pictures. She enjoyed looking at her own profile through these fresh mango eyes. She became methodical in liking pictures and commenting on stories and other comments. Sabine was horny for subterfuge. Horny for being rude to the world.

Again the sound of laughter interrupted her artistic process. The laughter, which had turned in the space of seconds to voices arguing, was coming from her studio. *Female voices?* Sabine refilled her wineglass to the brim, then carried it across the living room carpet. Around her the house seemed to warp and waver. The sun came through in such a way that every object around her looked pearlescent. She suctioned liquid from the top of the glass as she walked, careful not to trip in her Maseur sandals and fuzzy arctic socks, which now, when she looked down at her feet, seemed miles away.

She focused her attention only on the voices. They were arguing. The rising tones of two or more voices trying to be heard. Someone else shushing.

"She's here," said a voice.

"You tell her," said another voice.

"Shut up," said the first voice.

Sabine slowly opened the door. The room was still. She stepped inside. Nothing moved. The voices were silent. Sabine turned until she was facing the wall of puppets. All portraits of herself, familiar and foreign in the same moment. She looked at each face carefully. The puppets hung from their hooks, their eyes cast down at her, their mouths wide like suffocating fish. Sabine tugged on the feet of *Crone*, straightening the puppet against the wall. She did the same to the next, then cuffed the bottom of *Child*'s overalls.

Sabine sat at her desk. She turned to a new page in her journal and picked up a pen. With no distractions, she committed to being used for art. Inside her was an idea that she couldn't yet see, detached from the thread that held it under the surface of her mind. She fished for it. She closed her eyes and scanned her whole body for the submerged thought. She put down her pen. She swivelled her chair until she was looking at her puppets again.

An idea unfurled inside her. Turning back to her journal, Sabine picked up a pen and drew one circle on the page. She stared at the circle. *What next?* she asked her ascending idea.

"You're a pig," croaked a voice.

Dropping her pen, Sabine spun around. "Who said that?"

No one spoke.

Sabine rubbed her eyes and retrieved her pen, ready to document. Whatever new idea was making its way to her would clearly be a steaming-skunk badger-bite stonefish-poison thing of a piece. There was a simmering grandeur to it already. If she tried to ignore this pull, to compress the idea down into shards of slate in the pit of her being, then it would find a way to splinter her from the inside out. She wanted three things: to be bewitched, to be fit enough to endure it, and to recover afterwards. Every piece of art changed her, not always for the better. Carrying an idea can be like housing a parasite: it takes all resources, all energy. Making art is an athletic achievement.

"You. PIG!" said a voice.

Sabine spun around again to face the puppet wall. Her eyes fell to *Crone*, whose long grey hair trailed all the way down to pool on the studio floor. The puppet's legs paddled gently against the wall in the breeze. Sabine glanced at the closed window. *What breeze?* She squinted at the prosthetic face. *Crone*'s pupils dilated, her head jerked upright, and her mouth opened even wider.

"You're a pig!" *Crone* screeched. Her feet drummed wildly against the wall. Her prosthetic tongue fell from her mouth and thumped to the floor.

One by one, the puppets either side of *Crone* animated. Their eyes blinked open to focus on Sabine. She stood and tripped backwards, knocking into her chair.

"You fucking pig!" the puppets screeched.

Untitled (Pig Woman)

—CINDY SHERMAN, 1986

At the halal butcher in Brunswick, Sabine bought four pig feet for ten dollars.

"What are you making?" the butcher asked as he handed her the paper-wrapped feet.

"It's for art," said Sabine.

"Art? What type of art?" he said.

"Performance art," said Sabine. She put the package in her bag.

"You're not going to eat the meat? It's good meat," said the butcher.

"I'm sorry," said Sabine.

"What else do you need for your performance? We have shanks, shoulder, diced lamb off the bone . . ." He patted a side of bright red meat tightly covered in cling film.

"Nothing else," said Sabine.

"Tag us in the photos." The butcher pointed to the Instagram handle at the front of the store.

At home, Sabine took the package of trotters straight to her studio. She stood in front of her puppets and raised her hand, offering them the package. They rocked back and forth on their hooks, rattling their bodies against the wall. A ripple of relief passed through them. *Pig*, they collectively sighed.

"Am I the pig?" said Sabine.

No response.

Sabine unwrapped the long, pale-pink trotters and used a large needle to thread them onto long strips of leather cord. She tied a trotter to each of her ankles and then one to each wrist, tightening the straps until the trotters were secure against her skin. Sabine took a few steps wearing them. The hooves rested alongside her own feet, flush to the ground.

"Like this?" said Sabine. The idea was travelling alongside her.

Silence.

Sabine pulled out her tubs of materials, took off the lids, and stood over them. In one was textures—snakeskin, leathers, PVC, offcuts of fur, and vintage tapestries. A second held glass eyeballs, dentures, and bones. She had a handshake agreement with a farmer to collect the bones of deceased animals once they were dry. In another bucket were sockets and flanges, one flared hip bone, and a jawbone. She upended the rest of her tubs and picked through the contents.

Sabine made a mask that covered her, head to collarbones. She selected the most bulbous bones and arranged them into a face, then drilled two deep holes for eyes. She was crawling now, snorting and grunting while she looked for more scraps of material on the ground. From her box of bones came two long ribs from a cow. She attached one to each cheek of the mask, forming tusks. She pulled on the head, which completely covered her own. The mask was as heavy as a motorcycle helmet. The swish-swashing mane of her hair tumbled out of its bun and trailed from the bottom of the mask.

Sabine ran gleefully to the bedroom and pulled her fake fur coat from the hanger. She carefully inserted each of her huge double-trotter hands through the armholes, the silk lining cooling her prickling skin. She belted the coat tightly around her waist. *Yes.* She returned to the studio and stood, arms akimbo, in front of her puppets, legs in a wide stance, the coat tickling her calves. *Yes yes.* She undulated her body through the space and squealed, the weight of her mask making her turn faster. East of Sydney Road, south of the Meat Shack, Sabine stumbled down the hallway; her trotters clattering across the floorboards like wooden blocks.

This house wouldn't hold her long; she needed a pen. Out to a paddock. Out to run along rivers and sniff things up into her nostrils—oh! She'd forgotten her nostrils; she retrieved a conch shell, faced it slit out, and used Quick & Thick glue to stick it to the middle of the pig face.

"Oinketty oink." Sabine burped, she hiccupped.

"I am a piggy," she whispered.

"Let's get absolutely wrecked," said Sabine. She lifted the head briefly to vomit wine like a squeezed sponge.

Revenge Body

—EMMA STERN, 2021

"I personally love it," said Carolee.

The ghost of Carolee Schneemann stood in the corner of the room wearing the skin of *Adolescent*. She smoothed the braided wig and tucked the loose hairs behind the puppet's ears, which were lined with silver hoops. *Adolescent* was rigged with two full camel packs of vanilla-scented perfume beneath its school uniform. Sabine had spent months getting the mechanics perfect, and now every time the puppet shook its head, vanilla seeped from each armpit.

"You look totally inspired," said Carolee.

"I have a sudden need to bring him in," said Sabine.

She found a pen and opened her journal. Her fury reared up, excited. On a blank page, she scrawled: *The door is unlocked, come in.*

"And what is the plan after he's in?" said Carolee.

Sabine ripped the page from her journal with her trotter hands, which weighed down her arms like pieces of marble.

She read it aloud. "*The door is unlocked, come in.*"

"What about changing it to 'Come in, if you dare'?" said Carolee.

"Please don't interrupt my flow," said Sabine.

Carolee followed Sabine as she taped the note to the glass of the front door, then left it ajar. She took her time unlocking the back door. Moving methodically, making each action a small ritual, she unbolted each of the windows until the house was no safer than the rest of the evening.

"What does the muse tell you to do now?" said Carolee.

"I feel like I need to make space," said Sabine.

"I sense a performance coming. Is that what you're experiencing?" said Carolee.

The sun set as Sabine rolled the living room carpet away and swept the floor. She pushed all the furniture to the edges of the room and stood looking at the space.

"It's a stage, isn't it?" said Carolee, loosening her school tie.

"I'm thinking," said Sabine.

"As the pig or as yourself?" said Carolee.

"Both," said Sabine.

"Pigs are notoriously vicious," said Carolee.

Sabine ransacked the fridge, pulling out a plastic bag of lychees and a container of black rice, a soup bowl of soft red currants, a cut papaya. She took out a head of red cabbage and two soft leeks, then carried all of the food into the living room and arranged it in a pile on the floor.

"You have a menacing energy," said Carolee. "You bring a kind of darkness to the space that could be construed as primordial."

Sabine ignored her.

"Can you hear me? I said you bring a kind of darkness to the space that—"

"It's time to be quiet," said Sabine.

She tore open a packet of sausages and then swung them over her head like a lasso. She took eggs from their carton and rolled them into the living room, one after the other. Opened a bag of carrots and sprayed them across the room. Picked up a pomegranate, broke it in half, and threw it towards the record player, scattering the glistening seeds like Sri Lankan garnets. She looked for more meat. With her body half inside the fridge, she plunged a fork into a rose-coloured side of salmon and grabbed a greying shoulder of mutton under one arm, then added them both. She worked diligently, adding cassis, cracked seeds, crushed nuts.

Carolee inspected Sabine's work.

"This is a homage to *Meat Joy*," said Carolee.

"It's completely different. *Meat Joy* was erotic," said Sabine.

"If you roll around on this food, or play music, or have any urge to think of your body as being part of the work, it will be a reproduction, and I'm here to say, I don't mind," said Carolee.

"It's more of an altar," said Sabine.

"An altar to my work? An altar to piggery? To violence? What is it an altar to?" said Carolee.

Outside the back door, Sabine broke leaves off the agave plant, then carried the long limbs into the house, where they dripped and oozed sap across the floor. Spices and nightshades, charred eggplant, sun-dried tomato. On top of the altar Sabine splattered fistfuls of jam. She lit seven sticks of incense, put them at the base of the altar, and then selected a disco album to play on the record player, turning it all the way up until the speakers crackled and the volume became disorienting.

Behind the altar of food, she positioned the three-seater sofa. She then set up two tripods facing the sofa, one holding her phone and the other her camera. She had to document this seminal work. This could very well be her next exhibition piece. At the very least this was proof for Constantine. She pressed record on each.

"Are you live streaming this?" said Carolee.

"No. I'm just recording," said Sabine.

"The light is on like it's a live stream," said Carolee.

"It just looks the same," said Sabine.

She ran her tongue over her incisor teeth. She made fists of her hands to remind herself how sharp her filed nails were. Claws. She glanced down at her feet. Hooves. Slowly she reached her hands to her face. Tusks burst outwards. Billiard balls in a sock for a brain. What else did this scene need? A pipe organ. A choir. A round of applause.

"This is geopolitical. This is magnificent. We must not rush. No acting! Be in the now," said Carolee. She sat on the altar, spread her fingers, and drove them into the mound of food, then lay back and wiggled her body down into the sludge.

"You've brought us all the way here, into this absolute mire, for what? What is your statement?" said Carolee.

Sabine wagged her tongue from side to side. The words wanted to come.

"Hark," said Sabine.

"Not where I'd begin, but keep going," said Carolee.

"Hark," Sabine said again.

"Loosen your goddamn tongue, child," said Carolee. She raised her head briefly to throw a lychee at Sabine. A neighbour's light turned on.

"It is your duty to slam yourself against the wall that is blocking you from speaking intelligently about your art. You are the authority, so slam through and explain this all to me," said Carolee.

Sabine's throat opened. The words came as images at first, falling into the top of her head and rolling down her sinuses. Her breathing slowed. She placed a hand on her abdomen, shaking beneath her skin.

"You've invited a dangerous man into your house. Speak about it! Give it to me! Cleave to the bone, pig woman!" said Carolee.

Sabine cocked a leg onto a chair.

"What I want you to know about this piece of art is that it was made while I was rotting with fear." She stopped. The recording wouldn't pick up her voice over the music. She needed to yell. She lowered her leg from the chair, squared her shoulders, and started over.

Up went her leg onto the chair, again. She inhaled, pulled her diaphragm towards her spine, and readied herself.

"What I need to tell you about this art you see here, is that it was made while I rotted with fear. My bones dislocated in fright. My flesh abandoned me, falling from my skeleton like boiled beef, like slow-roasted lamb. Decrepit, I learned Latin. More botanical specimen than woman, I spored mushrooms and algae, I spored hate and fury, but mostly I simply rotted."

"You are a portal! You are an eternal spring! Let the fingers of the cosmos strum your bones like a harp!" said Carolee.

Sabine extended her hands out on either side of her body, embracing the scene.

"If that man touches me, my stench will cling to him. I will smear myself across his skin. Marks of tannin. Graphite. Black currant. Barnyard excrement. I'm a stain. An oil slick. I'm grease. If he touches me, he will shower and shower and never be clean. I am tattoo ink layers-deep under his skin. He is unable to digest me. I will change the colour of his shit. Supernatural, primordial, diabolical she. I am she. I am she!"

Carolee screamed, "You are sheeeeee!"

Sabine brought her hands in front of her face and admired her trotters.

"I have two slugs as lips, quandong-fruit eyes, a pomelo head. Out of my mouth rolls boiled eggs, choko vines, purple yams. Lay at my skeletal feet fetuses, durian, black olives, and persimmons still wet from the tree. I call to my side: screaming goats. I call to my side: planet Venus. Carnage! Violence! Rapture! Let a chorus of castrati accompany me as I burrow into the soft wall of his gut. What I want you to know about this piece of art is that it was always an arrow aimed at only one head."

"Time to get the skins," said Carolee.

Sabine fetched armfuls of her puppets from her studio. She set them in a seated position along the sofa with their heads flipped back against the backrest, each nose pointing to the ceiling. Accompanied by the pulsing backbeat of the disco music, she laid some of them to either side of the sofa and then brought the rest from her studio until all eighty of them were splayed out across the room.

Carolee sat in the middle of the sofa, a hand over each knee. Her eyes rolled back in her head as the puppets on either side of her inflated from their feet to their heads, until they looked alive. The puppets sat upright beside Carolee. Sabine stood in front of them, her eyes darting across the room, making eye contact with each of her puppets. She dipped her head in reverence, and they each dipped theirs in return.

Sabine opened all the curtains in the house, wedged herself between Carolee and her puppets, and they sat, facing the back door. To their right, beyond the large window that faced the garden, the Rembrandt Man stood watching.

Could It Be Magic

—DONNA SUMMER, 1976

The Rembrandt Man wiped drops of rain off the living room window, cupped his hands to the glass, and pressed his face between them. He peered through the window, scanning the dark room for her.

"I see you," he said through the glass.

Carolee stiffened next to her on the sofa.

The Rembrandt Man walked past the windows until he reached the back door, then stopped. The handle of the back door turned, and he stepped into the kitchen. Carbonated blood flicked hot bubbles through Sabine's veins. A buzzing lightness under each hair on her scalp. It was as if whatever was inside her was trying to split her open and emerge. An avocado pit shooting out a stem of green.

The man was taller than she remembered but thinner too, his narrow shoulders hunched beneath the rigid oilskin of his jacket. His vacant eyes at half-mast as he tracked each object of her altar. As if smelling something foul, he briefly held the back of his gloved hand to his nose, wiping it. Her body locked together as one frozen block. The mask and coat she was wearing were the only layer between them. The man lowered his hand but kept it balled in a fist. He walked from the kitchen to the living room, fixated on the sofa. As he drew closer his eyes widened. He looked closely at Sabine and then scanned across at each effigy. He raised his hand and wiped his nose again.

Sabine morphed. Fury and fear climbed up her legs and crawled over her stomach, and by the time they reached her chest she was blinking evenly, undisturbed. Next to her, a puppet hiccupped.

"Sabine?" The man turned his head to face her.

"What can I get you?" said *Waitress*, who was perched on the far end of the sofa. His head snapped towards the puppet.

"Take your mask off," he ordered. He clenched his jaw, which made the tendons along his neck jump then quickly drop.

"What mask?" said Sabine. The man wheeled back to look at her.

Waitress stifled a laugh.

"What did you say?" said the man.

"Nothing," said Carolee and Sabine in unison.

The man peered at Sabine's masked face. He stepped to the side until he could bend slightly to be on level with her eyes. She let him meet her gaze.

Being this close to him felt psychedelic. For days, she hadn't wanted to smell like anything artificial, so she hadn't used soap; since she had received the first letter she'd also stopped using deodorant, letting her own mix of pheromones and toxins bloom. Now, the smell coming from her body, leaching into the air between them, was carnal. It was ripe.

The man sneered at her, and a flicker of something else crossed his face. A microscopic fleck of wariness. The man took another step forward, towards the pig. He smiled.

"I see you in there," said the Rembrandt Man.

Sabine leapt up and screeched. Chainsaws. Metal grinders. Hot tyres on bitumen. Diamond blades through concrete.

"Dare ye speak to this here pig?" screamed Sabine. She put both hands on her hips. *Waitress* quickly stood on the arm of the sofa. Carolee moved into a cross-seated position.

"Who else is here?" said the Rembrandt Man, looking behind her.

"Just me," said Sabine. An oink escaped her mouth.

"Enough of this." The Rembrandt Man took a few steps forward and slid sideways on an agave spear.

"This floor is disgusting," said the Rembrandt Man.

"I will eat whatever comes into my pen." Sabine performed a conquistador dance while licking her fingers, one by one, through the mask.

"And then I will roam wildly," she danced thunderously on the spot, "over hills and paddocks."

The screen of Sabine's phone came to life.

YuletideHam commented: *I am so tired of seeing the same stuff from female artists fucking yawn*

Pretty_Kitty_Lover commented: *Sorry, what gallery is this?*

GlutenPutin commented: *Immediately no*

Ruthsexycool commented: *WHAT IS HAPPENING???*

GlutenPutin commented: *Freaky to see all her puppets en masse*

Ruthsexycool commented: *I'M CALLING THE COPS*

TheGoetheGalleryOfficial commented: *Opening night of Sabine's exhibition tomorrow, West Melbourne, check our socials for location and times. We look forward to seeing you all there!*

"Shut up," said the man.

Sabine squealed. She snorted.

Summoned, the row of puppets somersaulted forward off the sofa and rose to the ceiling feet first, as if pulled on strings. They hung suspended there, upside down, their heads thrown backwards facing the man, their eyes level with his. He took a step back.

"What are they?" said her Rembrandt Man.

"They're all me, baby," said Sabine. She kicked half a pomegranate at him.

"Tell your friends to stop," said the man.

"Stop," *Crone* said.

"*Stopstopstopstopstop*," the rest echoed.

The Rembrandt Man grabbed for Sabine, but her own hands were quicker. No, they weren't her hands, they were the hands of her fury. The hands of thousands of women, of a thousand pigs, of a thousand puppets. *Uh-oh!* Her fists were so fast. And, *and*, what exactly were her hooves doing? She was pummelling his face with the pig hooves. They were ghost hands. Ancient hands. Hands of the dead. The man yelled and tried to break her trotters from her wrists, but she was one continuous piece of marble. She shook him off. *Couldn't he see?* She was calcified rage. Her beautiful marble trotter-clad hands of justice around his stringy little neck. Cheeky hands. These fucking hands! Truly terrible. His eyes bulged. She let go of his neck and his head snapped backwards. He stumbled. He fell.

HahahahahaOK commented: *Going to tell my kids this is Marina Abramović*

Pretty_Kitty_Lover commented: *Love the moodiness of the piece*

Ruthsexycool commented: *I'M IN AN UBER*

HahahahaahaOK commented: *Not the pig trying to street fight*

YuletideHam commented: *Anyone else notice her art become weirder lately?*

The Rembrandt Man scrambled up and ran out of the living room and through the kitchen. He flew out the back door, but Sabine followed. He skidded along the gravel path, glancing back at her every few steps, and she put her head down and charged after him. She stopped when he leapt over the front gate and sprinted away towards the main road.

In the back garden, wheezing, yelping, moaning, Sabine pulled at the knots in the leather straps until her trotters were free, then threw them into the lemon tree, where they caught in its branches. She spun on the spot, giddy with power, while inside the house the puppets slowly deflated, then streamed, one by one, to the ground.

By Holding in One's Left Hand a Peacock's or Hyena's Eye, Wrapped in Gold, One Finds Success in Love

—*THE COMPLETE KĀMA SŪTRA*, 1994

As one man exited another arrived from between the curtains on the opposite side of the stage. If it had been a pantomime, the audience would have gasped.

"Sabine?" Constantine called out. He stood in the door-way, removed his key from the lock, and squinted as he looked down the hall through the opaque haze of incense smoke.

"I brought you some pâté," he said. In his fist was a bon-bon of paste in cling film. "Ruth is apoplectic. She's convinced you're trying to fight a grown man in our house. I told her that I just spoke to you and you were taking a bath!"

Sabine stopped the recording, abruptly ending the live stream, and then stood at the shadowy mouth of the hallway. She was alight. Surely he could see her flickering from there. Embers poured from her ears. Couldn't her own husband hear the crackle of her bones?

"What's happened? What's going on? What are you wearing?" said Constantine.

He stayed near the door, his keys shining in his hand.

Sabine walked to the record player and turned the music down a little. She moved carefully around the strewn food, hyperaware of her surroundings.

"I should have been here," he said. "What happened to your head? You seem to have grown. Are you wearing a hat? How are you feeling?" He took a timid step towards her, then stopped.

"Constantine, tonight I was immortal. I was godlike. The arms of a thousand people pushed through me. It was as if part of him fell and I picked it up and added it to me and I am changed by it," said Sabine.

Constantine walked down the hallway towards her, then stood at the entrance to the living room looking at her altar. Her skins were in a heap, their hair and stockinged arms all intertwined.

"Is this the direction you're taking the puppets? I'm going to need to unpick the genealogy of it. The house is putrid. Are you traumatised? Is that my salmon on the floor?"

"It's art," Sabine said. She took his hand, her exoskeleton face clanging and bumping as she leaned forward. She led her husband to the bedroom.

"I need you to accept this," she said.

Constantine gripped onto the doorframe. "I mean, give me a minute, and I will, you know I will."

Inside, she was a beast, whirring and burning. She remembered how the man had run from the house. Clumsy. Bipedal. Slipping and sliding over the gravel. Merely human.

"Do I look different to you?" Sabine turned slowly in a circle.

"Yes," Constantine said.

Sabine unbuckled the belt around her coat and took it off. She removed all her clothing but kept on the pig head and lay on the bed.

"My love," Constantine said, or perhaps she imagined him saying, "you're mythical."

Even If One's Head Were to Be Suddenly Cut Off, He Should Be Able to Do One More Action with Certainty

—YAMAMOTO TSUNETOMO, 1716

Constantine crawled onto the bed. He lay on top of his monstrous wife, his hands on either side of her shoulders. He pulled open the mouth of the pig until he saw Sabine's beneath it, and he kissed her. Their mouths fully open, inhaling and exhaling, one a scuba diver and the other a tank. In a rush, Sabine moved his body into her own. Constantine ground his hips slowly rocking into her, but Sabine was impatient for the frenzy to begin. She flipped her husband onto his back and rode him with the same frantic energy that she had channelled on their wedding day in the disabled bathroom stall at Piazza Now! In the Mariana Trench of his sweat and spit, and the slippery wetness of her body, the animal of Sabine became aquatic.

She imagined the Rembrandt Man between them. All three bodies stacked together until she and Constantine eroded the man into specks of dust. The gravel of his person exfoliating down to nothing between the slapping friction of their skin.

"What position is this?" Constantine huffed.

Constantine lifted her mask as if to remove it, but she stopped his hand.

"I miss your face," said Constantine.

"This is my face from another species. Imagine you are in the forest and you've found me and we are mating like this," said Sabine.

With renewed energy, Constantine positioned himself behind Sabine, held on to her mask as if it was a set of reins, and pulled it so far back that the eyeholes cracked open and the mask tore across the bridge of her nose. He flung the pig mask against the wall then dragged her effortlessly from the bed and onto the Persian runner in the hallway and then repositioned her until they were no longer people but two Butoh dancers. She had his ass in her face, and her toes in his mouth. Sabine was a sheela na gig clinging to the picture rail along the wall by her fingertips. She was a banshee squatting and squealing and squirting. Sabine was the universe expanding and contracting, and she wore all the faces of the gods at once. Lord Brahma. Demeter. Mars. Odin. Howler monkeys whooped. Camps of flying foxes swarmed mangroves. Waves smashed with a wet hiss against a quarry wall. Glaciers calved and collapsed. As Constantine faced her, knelt on the ground and threw her legs over one shoulder, Sabine raised her head from the floor and screeched louder than the approaching sirens.

The Mortifying Ordeal
of Being Known

—ELENA GARRIGOLAS, 2023

And there she was on the day of her exhibition, sitting in an aggressive amount of sun. Sabine had left Constantine in bed to come and have breakfast with Lou and Ruth, who were still in the process of forgiving her for the late night before. They ordered licorice tea and Persian love cakes, huevos rancheros, two croissants, and a stack of pancakes to share.

"I cannot believe two police cars showed up," said Ruth.

"Four cops," said Sabine.

"What did they say?" said Lou.

"They thought she had severe mental health issues," said Ruth.

"One asked if the house was always in that state," said Sabine.

"How's Constantine?" said Lou.

"Exhausted. Probably has a shocking headache from that

limoncello. He told me he was upset he hadn't seen it coming," said Ruth.

Sabine looked at her hands: they were regular hands. She touched her face: no tusks. Her body was her own again. She held her hand to the steaming mug of tea and left it there, feeling the heat. Normal. Expected.

"You're telling me the whole thing was live?" said Sabine.

"Yep," said Ruth.

"What did you rig the puppets up with?" said Ruth.

"Do you believe in ghosts?" said Sabine.

"Without any doubt," said Ruth.

"I'm on the fence," said Lou.

"It was mainly one ghost, Carolee Schneemann, and then my fury must have powered the rest like a turbine," said Sabine.

"I think the mouths were motorised," said Ruth to Lou.

"And what about gods?" said Sabine.

"Egyptian? Nordic? Hindu? Greek? Be more specific," said Lou.

"Absolutely not, there are no gods," said Ruth.

"Aliens?" said Sabine.

"Of course," said Ruth.

"Only dickheads don't believe in aliens," said Lou.

"Do you think art is a spell?" said Sabine.

"No, babe, we've been through this, art is art," said Ruth.

"If it's done with intention, then yes," said Lou.

Sabine ate a love cake.

"I'm sorry about all the memes," said Sabine. It was fair to say that she had inundated Lou with memes since the dinner party.

"Some of them were good," said Lou.

Under the table, Ruth squeezed Sabine's leg.

"Mormon?" said Lou, looking at a woman wearing a long corduroy skirt, walking past the café.

"Jesuit," said Ruth.

Sabine checked her hands again. Still skin. Still knuckles and nails.

"Zen Buddhist," said Ruth, turning her head to watch a topless man jog past.

"The tan screams Hillsong," said Lou.

"He's wearing a cross," said Sabine.

"Catholic," said Ruth.

"But who are we to judge?" said Lou.

They ate in companionable silence. Lou winked at Sabine, and Ruth squeezed her leg again. Occasionally Sabine felt the need to verbalise the strange alchemy of the night before, but words didn't serve the unhinged wildness of the event. Sabine focused on her breakfast, drank her drinks, and ordered more. As the waiter brought them a round of virgin Bloody Marys, Sabine buried her face in the bushel of celery and felt gratitude slow her heart, almost to a stop.

After breakfast, Sabine returned home. Constantine had finished cleaning the house, removing any trace of food from the night before. The sofa had been pushed back into position and her puppets returned to their hooks in her studio. Outside, along the side of the house, several garbage bags filled with food stood waiting for the bin collection. Without saying anything he had cleared away the debris of plants and soil left by the Rembrandt Man, and stomped it down into the green waste bin. He watered the remaining plants. He stopped once to say that the garden needed a prune anyway. He said it offhandedly. Like the decimation had done them a favour. Then he had opened the windows and turned the fans on to the highest setting, airing everything. Their home smelled like sugar soap and window cleaner.

Sabine showered while Constantine leaned against the vanity and talked. He told her he understood she needed time to mentally prepare but wanted to know what he could do to help. Sabine told him she needed a Reuben sandwich. *Is that all?* he kept asking. *I can't hear you, my head is under the water,* Sabine kept replying. Constantine made her a lemon and honey tea in a ceramic mug so big they sometimes used it as a vase. He kissed her twice before leaving.

After marinating in a thirty-five-dollar sheet mask, Sabine applied her makeup ritualistically, drawing her liquid eyeliner with an upward flick at the outer edge of each eyelid. Ignoring, as much as she could, her reflection in the mirror, which kept wanting to be seen. She felt an acute need to lock eyes with herself. *Not now,* she told herself, *but later.* She rubbed a roller ball tube of mandarin oil into her temples and wrists and then applied a huge dot of it in the middle of her chest. She dressed in a mohair crop top and wide-legged baggy tracksuit pants. Yawns rose and popped in her open mouth. She let them come, one after another after another.

"Carolee, are you as tired as I am?" said Sabine to her empty home.

When she was ready, Sabine set a timer for twenty minutes and then lay on the bed, focusing on aligning her body perfectly, feet together, arms straight by her sides. She pulled the pillow across until it was symmetrical either side of her head. She closed her eyes and gave permission for her body to dissolve into sleep.

"Carolee, we should nap," said Sabine.

No sign of Carolee.

In the kitchen, Sabine boiled the kettle for no reason. Opened the fridge and shut it again. She removed the peg from an already open packet of chips and stood looking into the middle distance for a few moments while eating.

"Do you want a chip, Carolee?" said Sabine.

In her studio, Sabine stood in front of her wall of puppets. She picked up *Crone*'s tongue from the floor and clicked it back into the puppet's mouth. Sabine stared at her wall of puppets until her eyes watered.

Nothing moved.

To Be Aware of Your Own Momentum

—KELLI VANCE, 2015

Suspended above the double doors at the entrance to the Goethe, the poster of Sabine was as big as a bus. This mild Monday night was actually the culmination of years and years of thinking and work. If Ruth hadn't been there to catch her, Sabine would have collapsed into the hedge.

Fuck You, Help Me
Sabine Rossi
Free exhibition | On now
Nocturnal gothic puppet portraits reimagined.
Artist talk and opening tonight.

"How do I look?" said Sabine.
"Lucid. Fecund," said Ruth.
Sabine leaned against her friend.
"Do I look 'on'?" said Sabine.

"In every sense, yes. You couldn't look more 'on' if you tried," said Ruth.

They neared the doors, which slid open automatically. In the middle of the large room beyond stood Cecily, cradling Feather in her arms. The dog's spindly legs pointed to the ceiling as Cecily scratched her belly. With her tongue lolling and ears inside out, eyes at half-mast, Feather's tiny body radiated bliss and laziness in equal measure.

"Thank Christ you're here, I was about to ring," said Cecily. "How're your nerves?"

"I'm on, I'm ready," said Sabine. Ruth nodded, backing her up.

Freya ran down the corridor towards them, shrieking and jumping. They embraced Sabine.

"Your live stream last night was incredible. Utterly outstanding. You've raised the bar for the exhibition," Freya said.

"I heard it was unusual, Freya said it was very textural," said Cecily. "Some forewarning would have been wonderful."

"It was an incredibly experimental one-off, never to be repeated," said Ruth.

"I love when artists play with scarcity," said Cecily.

"Let us walk you through the exhibition before anyone else turns up," said Freya.

They moved as a pod to the back gallery, where Sabine's portraits hung at the perfect height along the walls. At first, she didn't dare look in case the pain of their not being good enough burned a hole in her face or heart, but then she did look at them, and when she really looked, she saw that each was brilliant. There were notes she could have given if asked, sure. Cecily had hung them, in spite of her protests, chronologically, but Sabine was not in the mood to ruin things now.

Sabine touched the first label. She used two fingers to stroke the price of her artwork.

Ruth walked around the gallery, pausing in front of each picture. "I told you," she said, over and over. "I bloody told you."

The soundscape playing in the background intensified.

"Alexa, pause," said Cecily. The music stopped.

"These are very bleak, superb, sub-urban ritualistic landscapes," Cecily said.

"You are a superstar," Freya said.

Sabine looked around the room, dumbfounded.

"It's voyeuristic—very William Blake. Low-fi and subdued," said Cecily.

Freya took Sabine by the shoulders. "I'm going to give you two words, okay? Here they are: *surreal* and *sublime*. The only things you should be focused on are these. And here they are in context—are you ready? It is *surreal* to have a show this big, and it is *sublime* to watch your faithful audience interact with it."

At 6:00 p.m. the exhibition was officially open. Sabine stood in the corner, consciously breathing, while waves of people entered the gallery space. She watched as each group walked slowly past her works. Pausing, sometimes discussing them, sometimes ignoring them to drink the wine. The crowd was a current, swelling and pooling; their body heat warmed the room.

Sabine's parents insisted on taking photos of her standing between Cecily and Freya and then her standing in front of the sign for the opening. Her father said the nudity was not as offensive as he'd thought it would be. Her mother thought the exhibition as a whole looked like stills from a documentary on hybrid humanoids.

"Sub-urban ritualistic landscapes," Cecily muttered, and again later through the night, louder and with more emphasis.

More people poured through the door, and in the middle of the crowd was Constantine, his formal jacket folded over his forearm. He wore one of the silk shirts she had thrifted for him and his beard was trimmed. Sabine stayed put, staring at her husband as he moved slowly through the gallery to position himself in front of the first artwork.

Cecily sidled up to her. "What's going on? How are you feeling now?"

"Disassociating," Sabine said, not taking her eyes off her husband. "But not in a bad way."

Cecily inhaled. "I can see several critics taking notes. It's going to be a hit."

"Will it go viral?" Sabine said, gazing at her husband, who was moving on to the next artwork.

"After last night, it might," said Cecily.

Sabine raised her phone and took a picture of Constantine smiling warmly at her work. He slid his phone out of his pocket and took a picture of it, and so she took a picture of him taking a picture, and then another of him smiling at the picture he'd taken.

Cecily told Sabine she needed to say a few words, as was customary at all openings at the Goethe. As the lights dimmed and the audience quietened, everyone was encouraged to make a circle for Sabine. *Surreal and sublime.* Sabine held the words close. Cecily gave her acknowledgement of country, then handed Sabine the microphone. Surrounding her were the faces of many other artists. Her parents, husband, and best friend, all beaming at her. She dipped her head to people in the crowd. All the local artists and art aficionados who were at every opening surrounded her.

As the crowd opened up further to accommodate her, she realised that the artistic impulse could strike at any time and she needed to be open and willing to facilitate its disruption, whatever the occasion. In fact, the energy she siphoned from her current exhibition could be used to fuel more work. Art begets art, begets art.

Sabine raised the microphone to her mouth. The feedback from the speaker whined.

"You cannot wrestle with a pig," she said.

The audience stared back at her. Ahead the projector, streaming her film, clunked.

"Because you will both end up covered in mud, and the pig will love it."

Sabine locked eyes with Freya, who nodded almost imperceptibly.

"You cannot wrestle with a pig!" Sabine said again. Cecily blinked rapidly in shock.

"Because, you see, you will both end up covered in mud, and the pig will love it."

Sweat dotted Sabine's upper lip. Her pants stuck to her thighs.

"Why can't I wrestle with the pig?" she asked, hoping no one would answer, that no one followed an urge to join in.

"Because I am the pig." Sabine squealed loudly. "I am the pig!"

Sabine tucked the microphone into the waistband of her pants, lay down on her back, and oinked. As much as she was now arranged in a careful line, there was something circular about an oink. It lost all meaning as it came out of her mouth, her lips zipping back and forward across her front teeth. She lifted her legs until she was rolling back and forth like a beetle on its back. This was art. Let them witness greatness pass through her like a long piss. Sabine was hand-pumping the heart of God. Oinks came out of her until they both lost and regained their meaning, such was her level of commitment, her dedication to becoming lost inside the oink.

Ruth kept her phone raised horizontally, filming. Sabine's parents smiled, bemused yet braced for more. Constantine was the first to start clapping. He took a bold step into the circle, breaking the performer-audience barrier. He looked at his wife tenderly and with concern. Sabine stopped oinking and sat up. Constantine, her one true intimate, her venerated sacred being, stood next to her. He turned to the crowd and maintained his furious applause. The audience joined in. Constantine reached his hand down and helped Sabine to her feet.

"What a fabulous and surprising performance you have put us through," he said.

Sabine received the appreciation of the crowd with a low bow, turning in a slow circle, making sure everyone received a generous piece of her.

"And I understood every moment of it," said Constantine, pulling her towards him.

Body Electric

—LANA DEL RAY, 2012

If anyone had asked Constantine what had happened for him during Sabine's speech, he would have said that he had forgotten to swallow his spit. His lips were numb. In fact, never in his thirty-eight years on the planet had he ever been so enthralled watching something. Sabine had saved nothing for later. It was feral.

When she gave that speech, it *unravelled* him. Sabine had taken the pig saying—the one that he had quoted to her—and broken it apart until every single person in that room was the pig. She had handed him, with two hands, a chunk of time and said, *Here, hold on to this.* The moment was in him, and he in it. Watching her kick her legs about and oink so loudly, it was loud without the mic, it was unreasonable. But he got the performance. How he understood it was that her art was like a drawer of spoons. The spoons were spoons, but they were also not spoons. Sabine made the spoons into forks. Or they had never been spoons to begin with. He got that, *bam*, he got it. And it was an honour to finally understand it all.

His father had once told him that some people love to fight, and it had taken him only two weeks of being with Sabine to believe it. It was as if she gained energy from confrontation; it totally delighted her. He hated it. Her needs, my God, why did she dramatise everything? Why was she so stubborn and offended by every single thing? She frightened him. Were all wives like her? He wanted to go around the audience and ask the other married people. He wanted to tell them Sabine was his wife and see if they understood what that meant. Why had no one told him marriage was so hard? Why did people act as though clear air between a couple was the default? Every day a new exotic creature was given to him with no information, no dietary requirements listed. Then the next day he was given another. And then another. Macaw. Pangolin. Sloth. And now pig. Sabine was all of them. Sometimes two in a day.

He had never wanted to be married—it was a piece of paper and an expensive party—but it had been important to her. Twenty-five thousand dollars they spent on the wedding. That much money would have paid for six months in Italy. A deposit to start his own restaurant. But she had that thing that made her need it—what did she have? The childhood thing. An insecure attachment style. Shitty experiences with other men. And now a stalker, for God's sake. Sabine had badgered him to get married, and then as soon as they were, she fought him, tirelessly, for no reason. It was madness. One article he had read said that in heterosexual couples, women are like bears and men are like trees, and the bear scratches the tree and tries to push it over to see if the tree is strong enough to take the bear's full weight. And so he tried to be tall and strong like a tree. He imagined himself as an ironwood, but Sabine scratched harder and harder until he doubted whether he even wanted to be a tree anymore. She was a relentless sun bear.

And his job was like being in the pits of hell for hours every night, shovelling hot food into rich people, but then afterwards, when it was quiet, he missed the heat. He would go over the night again in his head, trying to remember it. Spent his whole life preparing for it, arriving to work early in order to prep, or to oversee other people prepping, or to fill orders or do inventory, or clean. It took a particular kind of person to know that feeling of being wholly consumed. Sabine loved the heat too, and art or performance or whatever he witnessed tonight was her heat.

Twelve waitresses. Before they got together, and even before they dated, if his memory served him correctly. If she asked again, he would tell her. No names, no details, although she would ask. *Twelve*. He practised saying it aloud.

"A dozen."

Constantine cleared his throat. He used his thumb and forefinger to apply pressure to the bridge of his nose. He definitely needed to say it more casually.

"If you were to divide them out over the course of ten years or so . . ."

It was important that he throw the words out there, with no hesitation.

"Sabine, it's only about one a year," he muttered quietly to himself.

He loved her. *He adored her.* There was no doubting it. No doubt at all. He didn't understand her daily needs perhaps as often as he should. She was unaware of any personal short-comings. He would also classify Sabine as quite sexually intense. But still, there was a deep, deep love there. Feral—that word kept coming to mind. His wife was feral.

Large and Small Form

—BARBARA HEPWORTH, 1934

On a post-performance high, Sabine went to her after-party and let everyone tell her she was brilliant more times than she should have. Her cheeks hurt from smiling. Her stomach cramped, and her mouth was dry from dehydration. The cost of being acutely receptive to the spectre of creativity. Sabine quickly became overwhelmed. Her skin was raw. She felt psychically injured. Making art and then giving it to the world was a mammoth task. She found it harder and harder to find the energy to thank people, let alone listen to their responses over the music. She leaned against Constantine but listening to him talk about pizza dough recipes with Lou was also too much. Ruth was grilling Freya and Cecily about how she could branch out from cakes. People shook her hand and she extended her own but it was as if a Teflon bubble had been placed over her; she couldn't really hear them or touch them. Occasionally, someone would bump into her and the bubble would pop and she would be exposed to the rough texture of a crowd and the deafening chorus of some outrageous song. She lasted an hour before leaving alone.

In bed, lying in the dark, Sabine pulled the covers up to her chin, relieved to be discombobulating in peace. The art had sucked her blood from her body and she was too tired to even remove her makeup. Her eyes itched but she couldn't lift a hand to rub them. Exhausted, she fell asleep briefly, but was woken only moments later by the ghost of Carolee Schnee-mann standing by the side of her bed. Carolee held a round tiered cake on a dinner plate. Scalloped lines of ruffled icing drooped in banners around the edge. Piped on the cake in a curly font were the words *Congratulations on Not Dying*.

"Thank you," said Sabine.

"You were lucky," said Carolee.

"I feel—" began Sabine.

Carolee interrupted her. "Feelings are fickle. Trauma, pain, all of it, blah blah blah. It comes and goes. Don't get attached."

"I'm so tired," said Sabine.

"Life is exhausting," said Carolee.

"Are you proud of me?" said Sabine.

"Proud isn't the right word," said Carolee.

"I let my fury wear me," said Sabine.

"It was art. You made something truly revolting and provocative and I can appreciate that," said Carolee.

"I saw an opportunity," said Sabine.

"Train yourself to see more," said Carolee.

"Is that mascarpone icing?" said Sabine.

"I don't know, it's shop-bought," said Carolee.

"Will the police find him?" said Sabine.

"Maybe, but probably not. It doesn't matter, though. He was the least interesting part of all of it," said Carolee.

"Will my show be a success?" said Sabine.

"Success is never a means to measure the quality of your art," said Carolee.

"Will you keep visiting me?" said Sabine.

"I don't think so. I deserve some peace," said Carolee.

"Are you my guardian angel?" said Sabine.

"No, I'm the ghost of Carolee Schneemann," said Carolee, pointing to her own face.

"Shall I get us spoons?" said Sabine.

"Our hands will be fine," said Carolee.

"Am I a genius?" said Sabine.

"Don't ask me these things. Let's just eat the cake," said Carolee.

Blinded, Ridiculed, Pitied

—JESSE MOCKRIN, 2020

A week later, Constantine used a long stick to knock the rotting pig feet, which had turned white in the rain, out of the lemon tree and into an open garbage bag. It was almost lunch but they had been gardening since morning in an attempt to return their home to normal.

"No one would believe it if you tried to describe the smell," said Constantine, gagging. "I mean how did we not see them up there?" He knotted the bag and placed it in the garbage bin. He sipped his iced tea, then unbuttoned his shirt and opened each side, cooling his chest.

"Art is a trick," Sabine said, again. She reclined across two large cushions she'd dragged into the sun. Next to her were a series of used plates and a sweating jug of iced tea.

Constantine pushed the wheelbarrow over to Sabine and let her choose what he would plant next. They were confident that many of the seedlings would not take, given they were heading into winter, but the act of planting something felt necessary. Sabine pointed to a beetroot seedling. He cleared a space next to her and made small holes in the dirt. He pushed a seedling into a hole, then repeated the action five more times until the punnet was emptied and a line of bright seedlings had formed at her feet. He then took a handful of mulch and blanketed the earth around them.

Since the exhibition opening, instead of making art, Sabine had been eating anything within reach. She scooped pickles out of jars containing floating peppercorns and feathers of dill. Crunched through thousands of seeded crackers, hundreds of banana chips fried in coconut oil. Used soup spoons to eat tzatziki. Consumed cheese, soft and hard, sometimes both at once.

"Eventually, I think you will make some fascinating art from these powerful emotions you are having," Constantine said. He watched his wife take a spear of cantaloupe and tie a slice of jamon in a bow around the midsection. She shoved it diagonally into her mouth.

"Art actually doesn't exist," she said.

"Okay, my love," said Constantine.

He asked her if seeing the garden being replenished helped her feel at home again, and Sabine replied that she wasn't quite sure yet.

Whenever Constantine felt the need to remind her that her mental health was better when she was making things, she permitted herself to reopen the pack of modelling clay he'd lugged home the day after her exhibition. Mostly, it was in a bid to appease him.

For a week Sabine had sat on the floor in her studio and sculpted figures. She smacked the clay together, moulding a series of females with big bellies, round bottoms, bumpy thighs, and padded feet. She dried them along the windowsills of the house, demonstrating that she had, yet again, given it a go. Once the effigies air-dried and cracked in the sun, Sabine walked along, holding out the kitchen bin, knocking them in, where they sank past onion skins and damp paper towels.

Mostly, though, Sabine had spent almost every day since the exhibition lying in bed, the covers up to her neck and a glass of raisins beside her. She munched and broke her brain further by watching TikToks obsessively. She followed women fifteen years younger than her as they paraded their Shein hauls for the camera. She scrolled through clips of parents singing "What a Wonderful World" to an ultrasound of their baby with Down syndrome. People reorganising their fridges with labelled, transparent containers. A watermelon being squeezed between the thighs of a female bodybuilder until it exploded in a mess in her lap. A nurse crunching into bell peppers smeared with cream cheese. There was an intimacy on this platform that soothed Sabine. She looked on at the world that kept existing free of her own torment, existing in the slipstream of more and more and more content.

Two days after her exhibition, a critic wrote a review accusing Sabine's spoken-word pig poetry of being contrived. *Contrived, boring, and egotistical.* Sabine reread it until she knew it by heart. The critic suggested, if anyone could believe it, that Sabine look at the work of Juno Calypso, and Sabine took to Twitter to tell the critic that she wouldn't know good art if it fucked her up the ass, but Cecily told her to delete the post and not to engage in any discourse because it looked graceless. Freya suggested that Sabine look into applying for fellowships and residencies, pushing her—just as Constantine was pushing her—to make more art. Who emails an artist with suggestions like these? The comparison of herself to any other artist caused a deep ache inside her. Sabine spent hours looking at Juno Calypso's work. It was inarguably, substantially better than Sabine's own work.

Constantine said that *Fuck You, Help Me* exalted the notion of women and nighttime happenings, and Sabine called her parents and Ruth to see if they agreed. She wrote a defensive essay called "Self-Analysis of a Self-Portrait as Pig," and sent it to several arts journals. No one ran it. Freya reminded her that accepting others' opinions was necessary, career-wise. Cecily told her that to be reviewed at all was a privilege. It equated to hype, which equated to sales, but Sabine was not above asking to see the figures. Sabine told them that what she really, truly wanted to do was to hold the critic by her ears and angle her pointy face back at her own work and say, *What, my sweet little, silver-spoon-fed, precious angel dumpling, is interesting about this absolute word salad?* But she couldn't. No one could. It wasn't allowed.

Most painful of all was that no one called her. Not one person rang and said the critic was wrong. There were no pitchforks and no fires to defend her honour. Sabine thought the silence would be the death of her. She rang Ruth and said that she was finally ready to hear Lou's opinion of her exhibition. She wanted to know his exact response, and if he saw himself in the work, but Ruth said they hadn't really talked about it. Sabine told Ruth how Cecily had described the exhibition as an impossible, defiant dream for people who identify as women, non-binary people, and trans people. *Did he feel the same?* She asked again and again, but Ruth told Sabine they had watched the performance and then left to get food before the after-party. "Are you actually kidding me?" Sabine said. Ruth told her to have a coffee and a shower and call her back later. Sabine waited forty minutes then rang again, and Ruth told her that Lou did not see himself in the work but had found the repetition of the oinks musical. Sabine was offended. "You're poking a bruise, Ruth," she said before hanging up. There had been nothing musical about it.

Sabine tried to bushwhack through the depression that was taking root in the fat of her brain. She ordered groceries online and then used every pot in the kitchen to make carrot cake with inch-thick cream cheese icing, lush key lime pies, chocolate mousse, like dark scoria, set in eggcups. There was comfort in the dense slowness of digestion. Ruth came over with the cake-decorating kit she used for her whales and demonstrated how to rotate the piping sack to make icing rosettes, but Sabine brought the piping bag to her mouth like a feeding tube and sucked out its contents. Sabine moved anything that reminded her of her art into black plastic tubs that she stacked at the back of her studio. Her journals, puppets, reams of fabric were packed away, a kind of forced custody. The only exception was a single notebook that contained too many stanzas of didactic poetry.

Art was dead. There was no mercy. No honest criticism either. Everyone was a tit. Everyone was drinking from the tit. Sabine told anyone who stood still long enough that she had sunk her teeth into the flesh of the art world's tit. She was sucking the hindmilk, she said; she had her leg up, kicking, and a fistful of its hair. No one was able to get any milk because she was gulping it all down.

"What exactly do you mean by that?" Constantine asked.

"I can't explain it any more than I have," said Sabine.

Cecily's version of damage control was to upload a photo

from *Fuck You, Help Me* to the Goethe social media account. It
was the only photo that depicted full-frontal nudity. The photo
was flagged and taken down. Cecily put it back up with black
bars across Sabine's nipples and pubic area. The censored
photo remained, but attracted half the number of likes.

Occasionally, Sabine found that the spirit of performance
did stir in her again, and when it did, she showed it respect by
listening. She pulled on a yellow paisley robe from the closet,
tying it firmly around her waist with a black silk sash. She slid
her feet into sheepskin slippers and squirted a drop of liquid
blush onto each side of her face, rubbing it into the apples of
her cheeks with both hands. Then she entered the living room
and took her spot standing behind her synth.

Sabine squared her shoulders and twiddled with some
knobs. She let the sounds of harpsichord and pipe organ drone
out into the mild evening. Constantine wandered inside to listen. Over the track, Sabine freestyled spoken-word poetry.

"Lost," she began.

"Leave. Art. No mercy. We are all lost."

Long pause.

"Mercy. Laughter. Pain. Death. You are nothing."

Short pause.

"Hunger. Thirst. We. Die."

Constantine shifted forward until he was perched on the
edge of the sofa, eyes closed and head nodding. Sabine impro-
vised some interpretive movement, rolling her shoulders and
letting her body slink through a slow grapevine. She stepped
carefully around and over the furniture in the living room,
darting her feet in and out of the hem of her robe. She kept her
knees bent and let her feet go wild, letting it become, for a few
minutes, a physical investigation only into footwork.

"We should record this," Sabine said, breaking character for a moment and trying to remember where she had shoved her camera. She kicked a foot up and spun gracefully in a circle.

"Just keep going," said Constantine.

But Ah, My Foes, and Oh,
My Friends

—EDNA ST. VINCENT MILLAY, 1922

Two months later, Sabine and Constantine sat at the dining table drinking the good bottle of Syrah from cut-crystal punch cups. A lit pillar candle sat in the middle of the table next to a bottle of Carolee's limoncello, while a funk record crackled on the player. In a silver dish, a whole smoked trout rested on a bed of leaves, discs of cut limes surrounding it like petals. Constantine deboned it cleanly with a series of folds and tugs that left the spine hanging from the head. As the needle moved to the next track, he stood and walked to the kitchen, his buttocks as taut as two goatskin drums beneath his pants. Constantine returned with a chunk of crumbling parmesan and a brown pear, which he sliced and then placed on a wooden cutting board next to the fish. Sabine added a handful of oily black olives to a ceramic bowl, and then washed a bunch of purple grapes in a colander before tipping them onto a glass plate.

"We've been through a lot together these last few months, haven't we?" said Sabine.

"A substantial amount," said Constantine.

The Rembrandt Man hadn't been to their home for weeks. No letters. No boot prints. No prowling in the night. No one had stood outside a window with the intention of breaking it. Sabine and Constantine had been in a washing machine filled with sand, both of them blind and disoriented, unsure of where they were or for how long, only for the cycle to stop and for them to be hauled out, to sit at this very table, listening to this very record.

On Sabine's lap was her journal, which she was using to sketch an idea for a new exhibition. She flashed Constantine the picture of a photographic series of herself, twisting in slow motion in a neon-lit pool at night. He loved it. He said she was extremely talented. Sabine grinned. She dated it, then turned to a new page to draw another idea.

"It's good to see you working again," Constantine said.

"I'm in the midst of a rebirth," said Sabine. She took a grape.

Constantine laid a piece of cheese on a slice of pear and then pushed it into his mouth. He slid his chair back and stood.

"Dance with me?" he said.

He extended his hand towards her. His eyes glittered. He smiled through each chew. Sabine closed her journal. He retracted his hand and instead danced backwards into the living room. Constantine swung his hips and rolled his fists through the air. Sabine said something like, *I need to get some air first*, or was it, *In a moment*, and then she very calmly—and with not an ounce of suspicious energy—left the room.

In the garden, Sabine stood near the fence line, facing the house. She watched from across the yard and through the window as Constantine continued to dance alone. In twilight, with the lights on, their home exuded a warm yellow glow.

Sabine saw her home from afar. In the bedroom, the lamp made shadows of the unmade bed, her clothes strewn from the door to the wardrobe. The tap in the shower dripped steadily. Each droplet splashed onto the soap scum that spread in milky arcs across the glass screen. The dishwasher flashed red, signifying the end of a cycle.

Constantine stopped dancing, walked over to the record, and turned the volume down. He scratched one forearm as he glanced around the room. He entered the kitchen and turned on the kettle, then opened and closed the refrigerator door. He returned to the dining table. Ate one olive and then another. He scooped a flake of fish from the tail and put that in his mouth too. He spun around.

"Sabine?" he said.

From where she was standing she could see Constantine walk down the hallway, pausing at the doorway of their bedroom. He kept his hands on the frame as he leaned in and looked around the room.

"Sabine?" he said again, louder.

Constantine turned around and strode into the bathroom. He stood in front of the mirror with his hands either side of the sink and looked at his reflection. Constantine ran the tap. He splashed water over his face. It dripped from his chin and he took a towel from the rack and patted his face dry. He dropped the towel to the floor, then opened the door and stepped into the hall.

"My love?" Constantine called out.

Sabine shivered. The night air was mild and soft. The sun had recently set along the horizon in one last burning line of orange.

"Where are you?" said Constantine. He systematically searched the house for her.

The wind had given up, and the rain too. Everything became extraordinarily still.

"Sabine?" Constantine wiped his eyes on his sleeve as he strode from one end of the house to the other. He looked behind doors. Opened the closet. Opened the linen press. Circled the laundry.

Her neighbourhood felt calm and still. A glossy sheen coated the houses and plants and pavement, everything having been washed clean by the rain. Sabine could hear the next-door neighbour's television, on but barely audible. Beyond that, the mechanical arms of the distant wrecking yard clanged as it pounded another car for three minutes flat.

Constantine opened the back door. "Are you out here?" he said.

Sabine ducked down until she was hidden behind the spiderflower. Her phone rang in her hand. Constantine's name on her screen. She quickly silenced it. He tried again, followed by a series of text messages she didn't open. Sabine watched her husband through the window, standing still, his phone held to his ear expectantly. She was transfixed.

Art emulated private things in a public space, but through the process diluted the original impulse. Here, though, Sabine was receiving the fullness of Constantine. She was a present witness to the true and only version of him, and it was perfect.

Her husband continued to call out, his voice rising shrilly. He flung open doors and looked desperately for his wife behind them, even sliding his sweatshirts aside to look for her in the closet, panicking.

Sabine retreated into the net of vines that hung over the fence, until they gave like a mattress behind her. She raised her phone, and pressed the record button, as Constantine sat down at the kitchen table and hung his head. He lifted one shaking hand to his chest, and rested it there, above his heart. Sabine used the zoom function to slowly pull her husband closer.

Works Mentioned

THIS IS NOT A LOVE SONG

00   Public Image Ltd, "This Is Not a Love Song," *This Is What You Want . . . This Is What You Get*, Virgin, 1983

00   Tracey Emin, *Rip my heart out You Fucking Cunt*, acrylic on canvas, 2022

00   Robert Burns, "Auld Lang Syne," 1788

A FIERCE AND VIOLENT OPENING

00   Dorothea Lasky, "A Fierce and Violent Opening," *Milk*, Wave Books, Seattle, 2018

MUTINY BY MAISON MARGIELA

00   Nadia Lee Cohen, *Mutiny by Maison Margiela*, film duration: 1 minute, 2019

00   Félix González-Torres, *"Untitled" (Portrait of Ross in L.A.)*, installation of unlimited supply of wrapped lollies, 1991

00   Chris Burden, *Velvet Water*, performance art where the artist

tried to inhale water, duration: 5 mins, School of the Art Institute of Chicago, Chicago, 1974

oo   Joseph Beuys, *I Like America and America Likes Me*, performance art where the artist lived with one wild coyote in a single room, duration: 3 days, René Block Gallery, New York, 1974

oo   Marina Abramović, *Rhythm 0*, performance art where the artist invited the audience to interact with her using a selection of seventy-two objects including a gun, comb, whip, perfume, matches, safety pin, lamb bone, honey, salt, and hat, duration: 6 hours, Studio Morra, Naples, 1974

oo   "Smooth Operator," Sade, *Diamond Life*, track 1, Epic, 1984

MEAT JOY

oo   Carolee Schneemann, *Meat Joy*, kinetic theatre featuring eight performers writhing amid meat, fish, poultry, plastic sheeting, and paint, duration: unknown, subsequent film duration: 6 mins, Festival of Free Expression, Paris, 1964

oo   Carolee Schneemann, *The Infinity Kisses II*, chromogenic photograph, 1990–98

oo   Carolee Schneemann, "Eye Body #5" from *Eye Body: 36 Transformative Actions for Camera*, gelatin silver print, 1963

oo   Carolee Schneemann, "Eye Body #11" from *Eye Body: 36 Transformative Actions for Camera*, gelatin silver print, 1963

oo   Carolee Schneemann, "Eye Body #26" from *Eye Body: 36 Transformative Actions for Camera*, gelatin silver print, 1963

oo   Rembrandt, *Self-Portrait with Dishevelled Hair*, oil on canvas, c. 1628

VERY PRIVATE LITTLE RANDOM POSSIBILITIES

oo   Chloe Wise, *Very Private Little Random Possibilities*, oil on linen, 2021

YOU SEEMED TO ME A SMALL CHILD WITHOUT CHARM

oo   Sappho, *Sappho: A New Translation of the Complete Works*, translated by Diane J. Rayor and André Lardinois, stanza 49, line 2, Cambridge University Press, United Kingdom, [620 B.C.E.–550 B.C.E.] 2014

SKINNED RABBIT

oo   Antonio López García, *Skinned Rabbit*, oil on board, 1972

NOW MUSES, AND MY GENIUS, HELP

oo   Dante, *Inferno*, canto two, line 7, Vintage Classics, Random House, London, [1314] 2007

PROTECT ME FROM WHAT I WANT

oo   Jenny Holzer, *Protect Me from What I Want*, text-based public art, 1982

SO SHUT YOUR EYES WHILE MOTHER SINGS

oo   Eugene Field, "Winken, Blynken, and Nod," FriesenPress, Canada, [1889] 2014

oo   HS News, *Killer packs of "alien" house mice eating world's biggest birds alive*, YouTube, duration: 2 minutes, 56 seconds, accessed 2021

REACQUAINTED WITH MY LIMBS

oo   Lulama Wolf, *Reacquainted with My Limbs*, acrylic and sand on canvas, 2023

TROUBLE MOVING ON?

oo   Issy Wood, *Trouble Moving On?* oil on velvet, 2021

I SHOULD NOT ALLOW ANYONE TO INCONVENIENCE ME

00   Emily Brontë, *Wuthering Heights*, Penguin Classics, United
        Kingdom, [1847] 1995

A COSMIC AWAKENING

00   Suchitra Mattai, *A Cosmic Awakening*, vintage saris, fabric,
        tinsel, beaded fringe, and tassels, 2023

WHEN IT BECAME APPARENT THAT BOTH MEN AND BEASTS
WERE WEARING THEMSELVES OUT TO NO PURPOSE

00   Livy, *Hannibal*, Penguin Random House, UK, [59 B.C.E–17
        C.E.] 2016

IN SEARCH OF THE MIRACULOUS

00   Bastiaan Johan Christiaan (Bas Jan) Ader, *In Search of the Mi-
        raculous*, performance art where the artist attempted to sail
        across the Atlantic but went missing, presumed dead, 1975

GLORIFY ME!

000   Vladimir Mayakovsky, *A Cloud in Trousers (Oberon Modern
        Plays), Steve Trafford*, part II, stanza 1, line 1, Oberon Books
        Ltd, London, [1916] 2005

THE GIRL AND THE GOAT

000   Cecily Brown, *The Girl and the Goat*, oil on linen, 2013–14

WHY IT IS THAT WOMEN ARE CHIEFLY ADDICTED TO EVIL
SUPERSTITIONS

000   Jacob Sprenger and Heinrich Kramer, *The Hammer of Witches*,
        translated by Montague Summers, Pantianos Classics, [1486]
        1948

WITH THE LAST VIBRATIONS OF HER JANGLED NERVES

ooo   Gustave Flaubert, *Madame Bovary*, Penguin Books, London,
       [1857] 2013

FEVER DREAMS

ooo   Laurel Nakadate, *Fever Dreams*, exhibition of photographs,
       C-print, Galerie Tanja Wagner, Berlin, 2009

YOUR LOVE TOUCHES ME, BUT I CAN'T RETURN IT, THAT'S ALL

ooo   Anton Chekhov, *The Seagull*, Signet Classics, New York, [1895]
       1964

NO FEAR OF DEPTHS

ooo   Patricia Piccinini, *No Fear of Depths*, sculpture from silicone,
       fibreglass, hair, 2019

PRODIGAL SELF

ooo   Eartheater, "Prodigal Self," *Trinity*, Chemical X, 2019

FOR FIVE MINUTES I CONSIDERED MYSELF UTTERLY DISGRACED FOREVER

ooo   Fyodor Dostoevsky, *Devils*, Wordsworth Classics of World Lit-
       erature, [1871–72] 2005

R U DUMB?

ooo   Jme (feat. Wiley, Cookie, and Tempa T), "R U Dumb?" *History*,
       Boy Better Know, United Kingdom, 2011

SHE WAS TERRIFIED, AND, ASTONISHED, SHE RECOILED FROM HERSELF

ooo   Ovid, *The Metamorphoses of Ovid*, H. G. Bohn, London, [8 C.E.] 1858

ooo   RAP GOD, Best Rap [fire emoji] Playlist To Break The Aux [fire
       emoji], Spotify, duration: 12 hours, 59 minutes, accessed 2023

THE LAST THING I SAID TO YOU WAS DON'T LEAVE ME HERE II

ooo   Tracey Emin, *The Last Thing I Said to You Was Don't Leave Me
       Here II*, digital print on paper, 2000
ooo   Dr. Terry Goldsworthy and Mathew Raj, "Stopping the
       stalker: Victim responses to stalking—An examination of
       victim responses to determine factors affecting the inten-
       sity and duration of stalking," *Griffith Law Journal*, vol. 2 no.
       1, p. 189, 2014

ORGY FOR TEN PEOPLE IN ONE BODY

ooo   Isabelle Albuquerque, *Orgy for Ten People in One Body*, an ex-
       hibition of figurative sculptures made from wax, bronze, wal-
       nut, resin, rubber, and fur, Jeffrey Deitch, New York, 2022
ooo   "Safety Tips for Stalking Victims," WomensLaw.org, "About
       Abuse," accessed 2020
ooo   J. Reid Meloy, *The Psychology of Stalking: Clinical and forensic
       perspectives*, Academic Press, 1998
ooo   Candice Sutton, "Shadowed by a killer: Jill Meagher's final
       walk," News.com.au, 2017
ooo   Whitney Houston FBI File, Paperlessarchives.com, 1988–92,
       accessed 2020
ooo   Robin Warder, "Ten Terrifying Cases of Sadistic Stalkers,"
       Listverse, 2014
ooo   "Sexy girl in white socks fucked by intruder," uploaded by
       Honey BooBoo, duration: 7 minutes, Pornhub, 2023
ooo   "Intruder entered my room and I ended up liking his cock!"
       uploaded by Izanykata, duration: 6 minutes, 6 seconds, Porn-
       hub, 2022

ooo   "Two lesbian robbers fuck," uploaded by 2girlshome, dura-
      tion: 2 minutes, 6 seconds, Pornhub, 2021

ooo   "College student fucks for her life when robber breaks in," up-
      loaded by Moasera, duration: 11 minutes, 42 seconds, Porn-
      hub, 2023

OUR HEADS ARE ROUND SO OUR THOUGHTS CAN CHANGE DIRECTION

ooo   Francis Picabia, *Our Heads Are Round So Our Thoughts Can
      Change Direction*, a retrospective exhibition of works across
      all mediums including painting, poetry, and film, MoMA,
      New York, 2017

SHADOW OF MEN

ooo   Cleon Peterson, *Shadow of Men*, an exhibition of murals,
      paintings, and sculptures, Museum of Contemporary Art,
      Denver, Colorado, 2018

TRUTH COMING OUT OF HER WELL

ooo   Jean-Léon Gérôme, *Truth Coming Out of Her Well*, oil on can-
      vas, 1896

TRIBUTE TO ANA MENDIETA

ooo   Tania Bruguera, *Tribute to Ana Mendieta*, site-specific re-
      enactments of performances by Ana Mendieta, Fototeca de
      Cuba, Havana, 1985–1996

ooo   Bruce Springsteen and Patti Smith, "Because the Night," *Eas-
      ter*, Arista, 1978

THE GUEST

ooo   Julie Curtiss, *The Guest*, acrylic vinyl and oil on canvas, 2018

SMALL BEASTS

000   Louise Howard, *Small Beasts*, oil on wood, 2022

DOGS WHICH CANNOT TOUCH EACH OTHER

000   Peng Yu and Sun Yuan, *Dogs Which Cannot Touch Each Other*,
       performance/installation featuring eight American pit bulls
       placed on treadmills facing each other and encouraged to
       run, subsequent video duration: 7 minutes, Beijing, 2003

TWO-HEADED

000   Tschabalala Self, *Two-Headed*, fabric, thread, painted canvas,
       acrylic paint, and oil pastel on canvas, 2023

000   The Beatles, "With a Little Help from My Friends," *Sgt. Pep-
       per's Lonely Hearts Club Band*, Capitol, 1967

UNTITLED (PIG WOMAN)

000   Cindy Sherman, *Untitled (Pig Woman)*, chromogenic colour
       print, 1986

REVENGE BODY

000   Emma Stern, *Revenge Body*, exhibition of portraits inspired by 3D
       erotica, women, and virtual reality, Carl Kostyál, London, 2021

COULD IT BE MAGIC

000   Donna Summer, "Could It Be Magic," Barry Manilow, Frédéric
       Chopin, Adrienne Anderson, *A Love Trilogy*, Oasis, 1976

BY HOLDING IN ONE'S LEFT HAND A PEACOCK'S OR HYENA'S
EYE, WRAPPED IN GOLD, ONE FINDS SUCCESS IN LOVE

000   *The Complete Kāma Sūtra*, translation by Alan Daniélou,
       Thomson Press, India, [fourth century] 1994

EVEN IF ONE'S HEAD WERE TO BE SUDDENLY CUT OFF, HE
SHOULD BE ABLE TO DO ONE MORE ACTION WITH CERTAINTY
ooo   Yamamoto Tsunetomo, *Hagakure: The Book of the Samurai*,
       Kodansha International Ltd, Tokyo, [1716] 1979

THE MORTIFYING ORDEAL OF BEING KNOWN
ooo   Elena Garrigolas, *The Mortifying Ordeal of Being Known*, oil on
       canvas, 2023

TO BE AWARE OF YOUR OWN MOMENTUM
ooo   Kelli Vance, *To Be Aware of Your Own Momentum*, oil on can-
       vas, 2015

BODY ELECTRIC
ooo   Lana Del Ray, "Body Electric," *Born to Die: The Paradise Edi-
       tion*, 2012

LARGE AND SMALL FORM
ooo   Barbara Hepworth, *Large and Small Form*, sculpture made
       from white alabaster, 1934

BLINDED, RIDICULED, PITIED
ooo   Jesse Mockrin, *Blinded, Ridiculed, Pitied*, oil on cotton, 2020

BUT AH, MY FOES, AND OH, MY FRIENDS
ooo   Edna St. Vincent Millay, "First Fig," from *A Few Figs from This-
       tles: Poems and Sonnets by Edna St. Vincent Millay*, Harper &
       Brothers, New York, 1922

Acknowledgements

I owe significant and ongoing gratitude to Grace Heifetz and Dana Murphy. Jane Palfreyman, Genevieve Buzo, Angela Handley, Clara Finlay, Jennifer Thurgate, and the team at Allen & Unwin. Kendall Storey, Elizabeth Pankova, Ryan Quinn, Megan Fishmann, Rachel Fershleisser, Vanessa Genao, Nicole Caputo, and the team at Catapult Books.

My deepest love and appreciation to Keith, Lulu, Nicky, Leena, Nellie, Megan, Paige, Susie, Anna, and Ben.

I am grateful to the City of Melbourne arts grants and Creative Australia for funding this work into existence.

Many of the artists cited have made art that has haunted me, but none more so than Carolee Schneemann. I am in debt to her experimental approach to performance and process, and to all the beautiful horror she created over the course of her life.

Finally, I want to acknowledge the person who stalked me. The fear and distress and fury they brought into my life has led me to make my proudest work to date.

© Mischa Baka

ELLA BAXTER is a writer and artist living on unceded land of the Wurundjeri people. She is the winner of the Best Young Australian Novelists Award and the author of *New Animal*, which was short-listed for the Readings New Australian Fiction Prize, the UTS Glenda Adams Award for New Writing and was long-listed for the Republic of Consciousness Prize and the Richell Prize for Emerging Writers.